TULIPS TOO LATE

A Flower Shop Mystery Novella

Kate Collins

TULIPS TOO LATE
A Flower Shop Mystery Novella
Copyright © Linda Tsoutsouris
All Rights Reserved

ACKNOWLEDGEMENTS

First of all, thank you to my wonderful readers. This series would not go on without the encouragement and support from fans of the flower shop series. Abby and Marco, as well as the entire cast of old and new characters, have become a part of our lives. We want to see them grow, want to see how they overcome obstacles, both great and small. We want to cheer for them. We want them to succeed. Through them we can safely root for love and justice.

Thank you for being a part of our world, and thank you for your continued support. As long as there are readers, there will be more flower shop adventures.

CONTENTS

Acknowledgements   Pg 4

Chapter One   Pg 7
Chapter Two   Pg 15
Chapter Three   Pg 27
Chapter Four   Pg 36
Chapter Five   Pg 44
Chapter Six   Pg 54
Chapter Seven   Pg 67
Chapter Eight   Pg 75
Chapter Nine   Pg 85
Chapter Ten   Pg 96
Chapter Eleven   Pg 106
Chapter Twelve   Pg 116
Chapter Thirteen   Pg 126
Chapter Fourteen   Pg 136
Chapter Fifteen   Pg 146

Dedication   Pg 161
Other Books in the Series   Pg 162
First Look –   Pg 164
The Goddess of Greene
Mysteries
About The Author   Pg 176

CHAPTER ONE

New Chapel, Indiana
April
Monday 7 p.m.

The sun was beginning to set behind the beautiful tan brick-and-stucco mansion as I drove my bright green *BLOOMERS FLOWER SHOP* minivan up the curving brick driveway. I parked near the front doors and took in the magnificent view. The oversized landscaping around the house and driveway was perfectly groomed. The second story was centered around a grand, half-oval window. Off to my left was a three-car garage, and inside the bay closest to the house sat a shimmering silver BMW with a vanity plate that said *Paige Me.*

This was my last delivery and I was uncharacteristically late because of a stopped freight train that had blocked traffic for over ten minutes, but I had taken that time to wolf down a snack bar, momentarily silencing my grumbling belly. I took the long white box out of the back of the van and straightened the bow. It was full of multi-colored tulips that Slade Rafferty, the owner of a successful realty firm in town, was sending to his wife Paige for their first anniversary. I shut the van door and carried the box up the brick driveway and across the wide cement porch to the front door. And there I came to a startled stop.

The glass window on the side of the door was shattered as though someone had put a fist through it, and the door was slightly ajar. With my heart revving, I stepped carefully around the glass shards that lay scattered on the cement below and called in softly at first, "Mrs. Rafferty?" and then tried again louder. No answer either time.

From behind the house I heard a car's engine starting and then the sound of wheels squealing on pavement. Alarmed, I fumbled with the long flower box, pulled out my phone, and called 911. After speaking with the dispatch operator, I took the box of tulips back to the cooler in the van, then paced up and down the driveway in front of the mansion, desperately wishing I could go inside to see if Mrs. Rafferty was all right. But having worked with my husband, Marco Salvare, a private detective, for nearly two years, I knew not to touch anything. It was driving me crazy.

Within minutes I heard sirens and then saw three squad cars race up Sandy Creek Court, pulling into the opposite side of the curving driveway. Sgt. Sean Reilly and his partner, Officer Bill Martin, emerged from the first car and immediately headed toward me. Sean stood at least two heads taller than me, trim in his tan uniform, with sandy brown hair parted at the side and deep blue eyes, and was never without a smoldering, inquisitive look on his face, especially when interacting with me.

Reilly had come to my rescue on more than several occasions, had pleaded with me to stop getting myself involved in harrowing, inescapable situations, and had even forced Marco and I to stop investigating our most recent case, to which we responded by solving it. But still, Sgt. Reilly had moved up the ranks of the New Chapel PD alongside my father, offering Marco and me the same respect and comradery. We had grown very close to Sean, and I was proud to call him my friend.

"You again?" Reilly asked sarcastically as he strode up beside me. "There's a surprise. What's going on?"

"I stopped to make a delivery and found the side light glass broken and the door open. I tried calling inside but no one answered." I pointed to the car parked in the open garage bay. "That's Paige Rafferty's BMW. She should be home."

"Okay, stay back," Reilly commanded. "We'll take it from here."

Officer Martin stepped onto the cement porch and sidled up to the front door. Reilly signaled for two of the officers to circle around the left side of the house, and the other two the right side, then used his elbow to open the front door wider.

"Mrs. Rafferty?" Reilly called. "New Chapel PD." Hearing no response, he tried again and finally said, "We're coming in."

He and his partner moved cautiously inside, hands on their readied holsters. I stayed back for a moment craning to see over their shoulders, then curiosity got the better of me and I crept across the porch, stopping just outside the doorway as Reilly scanned the enormous, high-ceilinged foyer and wide curving staircase, then proceeded cautiously into the living room on his left.

"Mrs. Rafferty?" Reilly called again. "New Chapel Police."

I stepped further into the house, keeping quiet and following at a safe distance as they made their way through the house and met in the massive kitchen at the back, where white countertops and black cabinets filled three walls, and a gigantic island sat in the middle of the room.

The aroma of coffee filled the air, as though it had been recently brewed. I caught a glimpse of a black marble kitchen table with white chairs in a large bay area in front of a bank of windows and that's when I saw Paige, her blonde head down on the table, a black and white coffee mug near her right hand.

Reilly used his shoulder radio to call for an ambulance, then slipped on latex gloves and went to examine her. He put his fingers on her neck and shook his head. "She's gone," he said to his partner. "Call the detectives and the coroner."

I had to turn away. Paige Rafferty, a beautiful woman who had once worked as a real estate agent at her husband's firm, was dead on the eve of her anniversary, her *first* anniversary, according to the note attached to the bouquet of tulips. I couldn't wrap my mind around it. Marco and I had been married just a year-and-a-half, and I didn't even want to imagine life without him. I had to quickly shake that thought from my head and stay focused.

When the other officers came through the back door, the first officer said, "The backyard is clear, Sergeant. No footprints anywhere but we found the back gate open and
fresh tire treads on the street behind the house."

Officer Martin stepped into view. "The sliding glass door here was unlocked and wide open. Looks like a quick escape out the back."

I couldn't keep quiet any longer. "Reilly, he's right. I heard a motor gun and tires squealing behind the house. I must have scared the killer away after he murdered Mrs. Rafferty and before he had a chance to finish robbing the place."

Reilly swiveled to give me glare. "Didn't I tell you to stay back? The house hasn't been cleared yet."

"First of all, I *am* back." Which I was, several feet at least. "And if you'll look over there you'll see what I'm talking about."

I pointed to a built-in desk area on the far-right side of the kitchen, where drawers had been pulled out and emptied onto the floor and a computer cord lay under the desk, still attached to the wall outlet, the computer missing. Paige's purse lay near the desk, the contents scattered, her wallet open, a tube of lipstick lying beneath the chair.

"I must have scared the killer away before he had a chance to finish," I repeated, as the thought really hit home. "And if I hadn't been stuck at a railroad crossing, I might have arrived in time to stop her murder."

As I said it and my words sank deeper, I felt sick to my stomach. But for that ten minutes, Paige Rafferty might still be alive.

Reilly must have noticed my distress because he came over and put his hands on my shoulders. "Abby, I appreciate your keen eye, but you've still got to get out of the way."

He turned back to his men. "Clear the house. McConnell, check upstairs to see if anything appears to be

11

taken. Smith, take the main floor. Beck, the basement. Keep your eye out for a cell phone."

"Are we looking for a weapon?" one of the officers asked.

"It looks like she was strangled," Reilly said, "and there's no blood that I can see without moving her, but let's not take any chances. Bill, start cordoning off the outside of the house."

Time for me to go.

As I headed toward the opened front door, with Officer Bill Martin right behind me, I caught sight of Detective Arno getting out of his car. I stopped immediately and feigned patting my pocket. "I must've dropped my keys," I said to the officer. "I'll be out in a minute."

As soon as Officer Martin had stepped outside to begin his task, I immediately ducked into an alcove off the huge foyer and waited for Arno to make his way to the kitchen.

In his early forties, Richard "Dutch" Arno was a senior detective known as the best closer on the force. He was an athletically built, tall, brute of a man whom I'd had the displeasure of meeting before. His hair was dark and slightly receding, combed back, just brushing the thick, upturned lapel of his long overcoat. He had a prominent forehead and dark eyes that could cut a person in half. I didn't like or trust him because of his narrow-minded attitude. Once he had a suspect in his sights, he went after that person with a vengeance even if there was evidence that pointed elsewhere.

It had happened to several people I knew, including my best friend Nikki, whom Marco and I'd had to prove innocent before she was charged as an accomplice in a murder case, so I was always on guard where Arno was concerned. Unfortunately, Arno solved cases fast, making the district attorney look good, and therefore he'd gained the trust of the DA as well as the Chief of Police.

As Arno approached Reilly, I moved quickly behind a pillar and then into a short hallway off the kitchen to listen.

"What do we have?" Arno asked.

"I'll wait until my officers finish outside and then fill you in," Reilly replied.

"Go ahead and round them up," Arno said. "I'll take a look around while we're waiting."

At that point the crime scene photographer, a forensic team, and the coroner arrived, so as soon as Arno left the kitchen, I took advantage of his absence, and a house full of people, to blend in with them and take some photos of my own.

When I caught sight of Arno coming back into the kitchen, I quickly tucked my phone away and inched back into my hiding place. Detective Arno joined Reilly and his men, gathered around Paige's body.

"By all indications," Reilly began, "someone broke into the house to rob the Rafferty's and murdered--,"

"Excuse me, Sergeant," Arno interrupted in his usual blunt, condescending manner, "but from everything *I've* seen, it's the exact opposite, a murder staged to look like a robbery. I'll pick up the husband and take him down to the station for questioning."

There it was, Arno's snap decision.

And here came mine.

CHAPTER TWO

"Wait a minute, *Dutch*," I called, stepping out of the hallway, causing all heads to swivel toward me. "Are you concluding that this is a murder before you've even listened to what Sergeant Reilly has to say? Why not hear him out before you decide Mr. Rafferty had something to do with his wife's death?"

"Who let Junior Miss Detective in here?" Arno snarled.

"Are you afraid to answer my question?" I challenged, as Reilly took my arm and backed me out of the kitchen.

"Questioning the husband is standard procedure," Reilly said quietly. "You know that."

"And you know how Dutch railroads the first person he sets his sights on," I said loud enough for the bull-headed detective to hear.

"Get her out of here *now*," Arno snapped, "before I arrest her for interfering with a police investigation. And

15

you and your men can leave now, too, Sergeant. I'll take over from here."

Reilly didn't say anything, but I could tell by the way his lips were pressed together as he escorted me to the front door that he was angry.

I stepped outside to see Officer Martin taping off the front porch with yellow crime scene tape. As Reilly lifted the tape to let me through, I said, "I'm sorry. I didn't mean to get you kicked off the case. That's the last thing I wanted to do."

He didn't respond, just gave me a look and pointed to my van. I nodded and started walking only to see the *New Chapel News* crime reporter, Connor MacKay, whom I'd known for years, striding over to meet me. He was wearing his usual white polo and khaki pants, a pen behind his ear and an audio recorder in his hand.

"Hey, Abby, I see the coroner's van is here. Who died?"

"I can't say anything until the family's been notified," I said as I sidestepped him and continued toward my vehicle.

"Then there *has* been a death," MacKay said.

Oops. I shouldn't have opened my mouth. "That doesn't necessarily mean there was a death."

"Come on, Knight. Let's not kid each other. I'm assuming it's Mrs. Rafferty."

I turned to give him a scowl. Instead of correcting him once again of my new last name, I simply said, "Go away, Connor."

"You've got to give me something to work with. How did you get inside?"

"I said, go away."

"Look, I can see Mrs. Rafferty's BMW in the garage and the front door has obviously been smashed open. So do we have a murderer on the loose?"

"You'll have to ask someone in charge."

"Great. I'll do just that." Connor smiled mischievously then called, "Sergeant Reilly."

I turned around to see Reilly stepping back outside. I hurried after Connor as he marched up to the porch, where the tape stopped him. "I was just talking to Abby and I understand there's been a death in the house. Is it a murder?"

"No comment," Reilly said, then gave me a glare.

I turned the glare on Connor. "I never said anything about a death in the house and you know it."

Ignoring me, Connor said to Reilly "There've been a string of robberies in this neighborhood over the past month. Would you say this could be related? Possibly a robbery gone bad?"

"I said no comment, MacKay."

"So you're not denying it, Sergeant?"

"What does no comment mean to you?" Reilly snapped.

"It means you're not denying it," Connor retorted.

"Come on, Connor," I said, looping my hand through his elbow, "I'll walk you back to your car."

"Thank you very much," Connor said, stumbling a bit as I jerked him forward, "but I can take a hint."

We had just reached my minivan when I heard someone call, "Sergeant Reilly?"

I glanced around to see Officers McConnell, Smith, and Beck step out to talk to Reilly. I immediately found myself being pushed around to the front of my vehicle so Connor could listen to them without being spotted. My gut instinct was to stop him, but my curiosity won out, so we both listened.

"The house is clear, Sarge," McConnell said. "We didn't recover a cell phone, but we found some interesting items that you should take a look at."

Officer Beck spoke next, "Detective Arno also informed us that you're turning the murder investigation over to him already. Is that true?"

"I'll speak with him about that," Reilly said. "Go ahead back to your patrols. We'll talk later. Good work, guys."

"So Mrs. Rafferty *was* murdered," Connor said, scribbling notes in his notebook. "And there *was* a robbery." He finished writing and glanced up with a Cheshire cat's smile.

"Don't you dare print that until you go down to the station and verify it with the police spokeswoman," I warned him. "Anything you heard those officers discussing is off limits until then."

"I wouldn't dream of printing anything unofficial," he said dryly. "And by the way, where were you when the murder happened?"

I glowered at him as I opened my van door.

"No, seriously," he said, laughing. "At least you can tell me if you were the one who found the body."

"I came to deliver flowers and that's all I'm saying. Goodbye, MacKay."

I was about to get into my van again when I heard a man call, "Hey, Abby Knight."

I looked around and saw Detective Arno motioning me over to his unmarked police car. I got out and walked toward him, with Connor on my heels. "It's

Abby Salvare now, Dutch," I said to him, "in case you hadn't heard."

"Sorry, *Mrs.* Salvare. MacKay, you get lost. Abby, take a seat in the back and let's have a talk, you and I."

I took a deep breath and slid into the back seat, preparing mentally to deal with a bully. Arno got into the driver's seat, then swiveled to talk to me. "I just wanted to say that you were right. I should have listened to what Reilly had to say before I commented. Can you think of anything else you noticed that might be helpful to the investigation?"

I was so stunned by his sudden change of attitude that I couldn't think of a reply. And then my inner antennae sprang up, waving a bright red flag. "If you really did listen to Reilly's information, then you wouldn't need to ask me anything."

"Okay, then how about a new question? How well do you know Mr. and Mrs. Rafferty?"

"Only as customers."

"I was told you came to deliver flowers to Mrs. Rafferty. What did you notice when you first knocked on the door?"

"Again, if you'd listened to what Reilly had to say, I wouldn't need to repeat it. I told him everything I saw."

I could see by the muscle tic in Arno's jaw that he was losing patience. "Look," he said, "I heard what you said to Reilly about me and I know you don't like me or the way I do my job, but all I'm doing is following procedure, as I always have done."

His procedure maybe. I looked out the window.

"I was wrong about implicating your friend before, too," he said, "and I apologize for that. I'm simply asking

19

for your input to help solve this case. You were the only person at the crime scene when police first arrived."

Wow. He was pulling out all the stops now. Still not saying a word, I glanced at him in the rear-view mirror and our gazes locked. His dark, penetrating eyes were working overtime, but I sat still. I wasn't about to be cut in half.

"So that's how you intend to play it," he said. "Okay, then listen to me carefully. I've made mistakes before, but I never make the same mistake twice. You can count on that. You're free to go."

I got out of the car, slammed the door, and walked away. No matter what he said, I would never trust him or his methods of working.

I heard him open his car door and call my name. "One more thing, Mrs. Salvare."

I turned around to glare at him. "What's that, Dutch?"

"Like I said before, you were the only person at the crime scene when police arrived."

"Yeah, what's your point?"

"Just that you should be thanking me."

"For?"

"For not railroading the first person I set my sights on." Arno gave me a smile that sent shivers down my spine. "Have a good day, Mrs. Salvare."

My phone rang as I got into the minivan and Marco's name popped up on the screen. "Hey, sunshine, it's after seven o'clock. I thought you had one delivery to make and were going to head home."

"I did have one delivery to make, or at least I tried to make the delivery."

I filled Marco in on what had had happened as I drove back to Bloomers to drop off the minivan and pick up my car. "I know Arno's way of working, Marco. He was actually trying to intimidate *me*, implying I had something to do with the murder. Now he's decided to target Mr. Rafferty. If *we* were investigating —"

"Okay, stop right there. We're *not* investigating, sweetheart, and you're probably starving. I'm drizzling the vinaigrette on our salads as we speak. So try to put what happened out of your mind and think about dinner instead."

Right. Just put it out of my mind. As if it were that easy. And salad is *not* dinner.

"How about pulled pork sandwiches instead?" I asked. "I can pick some up on the way home."

"We agreed to have a healthy salad for dinner, Sunshine."

"Fine," I said. "I'll be home soon."

I pulled into the garage, pushed the button on the remote garage door opener, and walked into the kitchen, still going over the events in my mind. There was something about that crime scene inside the Rafferty's kitchen that seemed off. I just couldn't put my finger on what that was.

. . .

Tuesday

I woke to the dull ache of sore muscles, making every subtle movement sheer agony. My stomach was running on salad fumes, and I could hear Marco playing with our pets in the living room without a care in the world. I touched my bare toes to the carpet and stood slowly, stretching my back and catching my reflection in our tall bedroom wall mirror. I pulled my chin into my neck and let my belly relax. This was going to be the hardest three weeks of my life.

The previous week, Marco and I had started our new exercise routine. The long, cold winter had definitely not been kind to me, and it was showing big time. Even as I had been loosening my belt and wearing larger clothes, the thought of eating better and working out hadn't really hit until we got the news.

My parents, along with Jillian's parents, had pooled together and surprised the family with cruise tickets to the Caribbean islands. The excitement soon wore off, though, when I began going through my summer clothes, and desperation quickly sank in when I tried on my old bathing suit. Marco had found me crying in the bathroom and decided that we would immediately start a strict healthy regiment to make sure we were both in great shape for our family vacation.

I pulled my stomach flat and straightened my shoulders, every muscle pulsing with pain. Caribbean cruise, here I come.

I was still musing over the murder when I sat down at breakfast. Marco was already exercising in the basement, and the newspaper was unfolded on the kitchen counter with the banner headline that read: MURDER ON SANDY CREEK COURT. Beneath was a photo of Paige Rafferty and below that was Connor MacKay's article. I made myself a breakfast of almond butter on toast, poured a cup of coffee - without creamer, ugh - and sat down to read it.

Paige Rafferty, forty-two, of New Chapel, Indiana, was found dead in her home yesterday. According to Police Sergeant Sean Reilly, Mrs. Rafferty was a victim of an apparent robbery/homicide.

My stomach gave a lurch when I saw Reilly's name, hoping Connor had verified that information as he'd promised.

I read on:

The victim's husband Slade Rafferty, owner of Rafferty Exclusive Homes Realty Company, is being held for questioning and is considered a person of interest. The investigation is now being led by Detective Richard Arno who will be making an official announcement tomorrow morning concerning the case.

I pushed the paper aside and went to the sink to rinse my cup, sickened all over again at the thought of how Arno would mess up the investigation. Marco came upstairs just then, looking as sexy and as masculine as always. He had a sheen of sweat on his face and his wavy dark hair was pushed away from his forehead. His soulful brown eyes brightened when he saw me, until he noticed the scowl on my face. "What's up, Buttercup? Ready for our workout?"

"Did you read the article about Slade Rafferty?"

"Yep."

"Is it normal for a detective to dismiss the first responding officers and take over the case?"

"It depends," Marco said. "Arno has experience. Although detective is technically the same rank as officer, a senior detective usually pulls a little more weight. It's not normal for a detective to dismiss his sergeant though, that I can tell you."

My handsome hubby knew what he was talking about. After serving two years as an Army Ranger, he'd spent a year on the police force before deciding he didn't like all the rules and regulations, so he'd bought Down the Hatch Bar and Grill and then set up his own private detective agency.

"That's what I thought, and it's another reason I don't trust Dutch."

"What happened is a tragedy, but it's not our case." Marco put his hands on my shoulders. "If we don't get a move on it, we're going to be late for work."

As I started toward the basement I continued, "I'll bet you anything he's not going to look at anyone other than Slade Rafferty."

"Not our case," Marco replied.

. . .

When I arrived at Bloomers that morning, my staff had already gathered to discuss business in the coffee-and-tea parlor, a former storage room that I'd transformed as a way to draw in more customers. Lottie Dombowski, the former owner of the flower shop, Grace Bingham, the ex-pat Brit who ran the coffee-and-tea parlor, and Rosa Marin, my newest employee, were suspiciously quiet as I entered the room. Grace stood to pour me a cup of her gourmet coffee, and as soon as I sat down with them, the discussion erupted into Paige Rafferty's murder and they began to fire questions at me about the delivery I'd made there.

Grace finally held up her hands. "Would everyone please give Abby a chance to speak?"

Grace was sixty-something, a widow, trim, with short, stylish gray hair. Physically fit, she climbed stairs without breaking a sweat and maintained her calm in any crisis. Today she was dressed in a pale blue sweater set, black pencil skirt, and sensible black flats.

I'd met Grace when she'd worked as legal secretary to Dave Hammond, a defense attorney where I'd interned during the disastrous year I spent in law school, the highlight of which was flunking out. But like anything else, something good had come out of it. I'd found my calling at Bloomers and met the man of my dreams shortly thereafter.

I filled my employees in on the details, including that Detective Arno – or, Dutch, as I condescendingly called him - had taken control of the investigation, and that Slade Rafferty had been picked up for questioning and labeled a person of interest, which for Dutch meant his top suspect.

"Still," Rosa said, flipping back her beautiful dark brown hair, "you cannot discount Mr. Rafferty." As usual, she had on a bright print blouse, this one off-the shoulders, and a flirty skirt with mile high heels. How she worked in them all day was beyond me. "I've seen too many shows on the TV where the husband looks innocent but, in the end" –she made a cutting motion across her throat— "guilty."

"Oh, you should have been here when he bought those tulips, Rosa," Lottie said. "He was all smiles,

25

blushing like a school boy when he made that order. I just don't think he has it in him."

"Rosa may have a point," Grace said as she poised herself. "As Aesop once noted, 'Beware lest you lose substance by grasping at the shadow.'"

I sat in silence, enjoying every sip of Grace's coffee, already mixed with my favorite heavy cream, (*oops*) while the women went back and forth on Slade Rafferty's guilt.

"Well, my dears," Grace finalized, "We must agree to disagree for the moment. It's nearly opening time."

We left the discussion there to get on with the morning's work. I pulled my first order, an arrangement for a tenth anniversary that the husband wanted all in pink, his wife's favorite colors. I stepped into the big cooler where we kept our stock and pulled pink roses, sweet peas, and peonies in shades of blush, pink and cerise, added some bright green honey bracelet with its thin needles and long flowing branches for contrast, then found a crackle-finish cream-colored ceramic vase and began to put it together.

But as I worked, I kept going over that kitchen scene in my mind. Something was nagging at me. I just couldn't figure out what that something was.

CHAPTER THREE

Marco and I had just finished supper that evening and were sitting at the table having a glass of wine when the doorbell rang. Marco went to answer it and I heard, "Come on in."

"Sorry to bother you at dinner time."

"No problem, Sean. You know you're always welcome."

Sean Reilly, dressed in a casual button-down shirt and tan pants, followed Marco into the dining area off the kitchen, looking as down in the mouth as I'd ever seen him. His thick jawline had the inkling of a five o' clock shadow and the worries lines around his forehead sunk deep into his skin. For a man who had recently proposed to the woman of his dreams, it was shocking to see him so distressed.

"Hi, Reilly. Have a seat," I said. "Would you like some coffee or a glass of wine?"

"No, thanks," he said, settling his big frame onto a chair at the kitchen table.

"Whiskey?" Marco offered.

"I don't think my stomach could handle it." Reilly took a deep breath and blew it out. "I'm in some pretty hot water and I need your help."

Marco sat down across from Reilly, "Anything you need, just ask."

Reilly gave Marco a nod. "Thank you. I don't want to involve you in a personal matter, but the truth is, my hands are tied and there's no one else I can turn to."

Reilly very seldom spoke of his personal life. It was only last week when he finally stopped by Down The Hatch to break the news to Marco about his engagement.

Marco leaned forward. "What's going on, Sean?"

"Let me start at the beginning."

He filled Marco in on all the details of the murder just as I remembered them and then said, "Before I left the Rafferty home, I went back to Detective Arno with the information my men had gathered. He said he was already on top of it and made it perfectly clear that I should butt out. So I calmly reminded him who was in charge and that I was going to have to speak with the captain before handing over the investigation.

"When I got back to the station, I spoke with Captain Fontaine about Arno's behavior but he brushed it off. Shortly after that, one of my men saw Arno going into the captain's office. Next thing I knew, I was being chewed out by Fontaine for jeopardizing Arno's investigation, and assigned to desk duty.

"That was yesterday," Reilly continued. "Then today, because of MacKay's article in *The New Chapel News,* I was called back into the captain's office and threatened with administrative leave because I'd leaked information to the press, once again jeopardizing the case."

I wanted to slink down into my chair. I should've stopped Connor from eavesdropping on that conversation. But I hadn't because I was listening, too.

"Arno is blaming me for the DA's reluctance to hold Slade Rafferty without bond. Because I was supposedly quoted as saying *Mrs. Rafferty was a victim of an apparent robbery/homicide,* there wasn't enough evidence to indict. Of course, Fontaine agreed with Arno and now I'm one wrong move away from administrative leave."

"I'll vouch for you, Reilly." And I was going to wring Connor's neck for what he wrote. "I know you didn't leak any information. I'll go to the chief of police if I have to."

"Don't do that," Reilly said. "Arno's arrest record is the only reason the chief still has a job." Reilly dropped his head into his hands and pulled his fingers through his hair.

"What do you want us to do?" I asked.

"I have information," Sean started. "My men found several suspicious items that Arno didn't even look at. These leads need to be investigated, but I can't go anywhere near this and I can't instruct my officers to either."

Marco rose from the table and grabbed his empty wine glass. "You've come to the right place."

"But this has to be done very quietly," Sean said, causing Marco to pause. "If Arno gets wind of a separate investigation he'll link it to me and I'll lose my job. I'll be done."

"We can be quiet," Marco said on his way to the kitchen. "Can't we, Sunshine?"

Three things I knew: I was partially responsible for Reilly's predicament; he was an honest police officer who didn't deserve to lose his career; and I would do whatever it took to help save it. I leaned in closer to Reilly and whispered, "Quite as a mouse."

Smiling for the first time that evening, Reilly said with a firm voice, "I don't know how to thank you."

"You've helped us many times over," Marco said, returning to the table with a fresh glass of Merlot and a glass of water for Reilly. "There's no need to thank us."

"Let's get started," I said eagerly. "What information did your men find?"

Reilly held the glass of water in his hands and stared at it while he relayed the information. "The Rafferty's back yard is enclosed by a large wooden gate. There was no lock on the gate, which I find very strange, and it was left wide open. Beyond the gate is a service road that runs along the back yards of all those fancy homes. On the side of the road they found several small diamonds scattered on the ground. They were right next to the tire tracks where the suspect presumably peeled away."

"I heard tires squealing after I knocked on the Rafferty's front door," I said. "Those diamonds must be related to the murder."

"Possibly," Reilly said, "but there's more puzzle pieces that don't fit. The side window by the front door was smashed and the door was open. My officers also found a paper grocery bag full of apples in the bushes next to the gate enclosing the backyard, but the gate was locked from the inside."

"A bag full of apples," I repeated.

"Apples," Reilly said again. "So we have a crime scene with two possible points of entry; one in the front and one in the back. Now, Arno wants this case closed quickly. He's sticking to the murder theory and he's going after Mr. Rafferty in full force."

"Isn't that normal?" Marco asked.

"Questioning the spouse first is normal procedure, yes, but it's more complicated than that," Reilly said. "Arno has positioned himself perfectly. Either Rafferty goes down for this murder or I go down for jeopardizing the case. Either way Arno wins."

"What's the deal with you two?" I probed. "Why all the animosity?"

"It's a long story. I won't bore you with the politics but let me assure you that Arno would be more than happy to see me leave the force. That's why I need you to solve this case before he does."

"Let's say for a moment that Rafferty did kill his wife," Marco said. "What then?"

"If he's guilty then all of this goes away," Reilly said. "My desk duty will expire and I'll be back to work, but I don't think Rafferty did it. I had a strange feeling about that crime scene. Something's not right."

"I had that same feeling." I pulled out my cell phone. "Let me show you some photos I took. There's something off but I can't figure out what it is."

"How did you get photos?" Reilly asked.

I paused to take a sip of wine.

31

"You never listen," Reilly said, normally giving me a stern glare, but this time he just shook his head playfully. "Let's take a look."

I grabbed my laptop from the kitchen counter, transferred the photos from my phone to the computer and pulled them up. I swiveled the screen to show Marco and Reilly. They took their time scrolling and studying the digital photos.

Marco stopped and enlarged one of images. "Look at her left hand. She's wearing a diamond wrist watch."

"That's it!" I exclaimed, suddenly realizing what I hadn't noticed this whole time.

"The watch?" Reilly asked.

"No," I said. "Her wedding ring is missing."

Reilly squinted at the pixelated image. "Why would the killer take the ring but leave the watch?"

"Maybe he ran out of time," Marco interjected with a wry smile.

"Seriously," I said. "Do you think the diamonds found in the road could be from her ring?"

"It's possible," Reilly answered. "See if you can find out what kind of ring Paige wore."

I made a mental note and moved on. "Here's the other thing I noticed," I said, pointing to the coffee mug near her right hand. "Look at this shot of the kitchen counter behind her. See the mug stand? Two mugs are gone but only one is on the table. Could she have been having coffee with someone who then attacked her?"

"That's making quite a leap, Sunshine," Marco said. "Maybe her husband used the mug that morning and stuck it in the dishwasher."

"Marco," I replied, "when was the last time you put your mug in the dishwasher before we left for work?"

Marco responded by not responding.

Reilly tapped his temple. "Abby might be onto something here. There was a fresh aroma of coffee in the air and one of the kitchen chairs had been pulled out next to Paige. The coffee mug could be an important piece of evidence." He leaned back, stretching out his legs, the confident Sergeant I remembered starting to come forth. "I'd recommend you two canvass the neighborhood, find out if anyone stopped by for coffee or saw anything unusual. That's what I'd have had my men do."

Turning to Reilly I asked, "I know it's a crime scene but is there any way we can get into the house to take a look around, maybe see what's inside the dishwasher?"

"Not until the detectives finish with it," Reilly said. "But I'm sure forensics would've confiscated the mug already. I suggest you pay a visit to Mr. Rafferty. He had a bond hearing this morning and was released this afternoon. Find out as much as you can while he's free but keep your eye out for Arno. We don't want any more trouble."

As we scrolled through the photos, Marco pointed to something I hadn't noticed. "See the shattered side light on the front door? If someone had smashed in the glass to unlock the door, the glass would be on the inside not the outside."

Reilly agreed. "And the door was unlocked. So Arno could be right. It seems as though someone wanted us to think it was a robbery first and a murder after the fact."

"But I arrived and interrupted the killer before he could finish staging the robbery," I said and closed my laptop.

Marco tapped his chin thoughtfully. "Whoever killed Paige must have fled through the back door where the car was already waiting, which indicates premeditation. But if the killer didn't break in, then Paige either invited the person inside or was forced to do so."

"You're on the right track," Reilly explained. "It seems to me like she had invited this person inside willingly."

"Then Paige must have known the person who murdered her," I said.

"There weren't any obvious signs of a struggle," Reilly added. "It's almost as if the killer walked up right behind her and grabbed her around the throat." He strangled his glass of water for effect.

"So we have to figure out who Paige would feel comfortable letting in her house and possibly even having coffee with." Marco looked at me. "We'll need to speak with Mr. Rafferty about that."

"That's what I would do," Sean said, brimming with confidence for the first time that evening.

"So we question Slade Rafferty, find out what kind of ring Paige wore, and canvass the neighborhood," I said. "Anything else?"

"You could figure out why a whole bag of apples were tossed in the bushes," Reilly said.

"We're on it, Sean," Marco concluded, standing up. "I'm going to get Abby a refill. Want some more water?"

Reilly also got up with a groan, rubbing his neck. "No thanks. I've got to get home and try to relax. If you find out anything, please call me, day or night. And Abby, I never thought I'd be saying this, but thank God you don't listen to me or we wouldn't have those photos."

"You're welcome," I said with a smile.

Before he walked out the door, Reilly turned to us, "I did have one other thought on the way over here."

"What's that?" I asked.

"I could just drop the case, look the other way, let my desk duty expire and return to work. It would be a whole heck of a lot easier."

"You could," Marco said. "But you didn't join the force because it was easy."

"No, but if I get put on administrative leave it would ruin my career. I don't know what else I would do. How could I start a family?"

"Have you told Marie yet?"

"How can I tell my fiancé that I might lose my job?"

"You won't lose your job, Sean," I stated firmly. "Team Salvare is on the case."

Reilly didn't say a word. He looked at both of us with a proud expression and, for the first time ever, I noticed a film of tears forming over his eyes. He nodded and slowly turned around to head for his car.

"Okay, Sunshine," Marco, said, locking the door. He grabbed the wine from the kitchen island. "Let's figure out our game plan for tomorrow."

I watched Marco top off my glass with the last few drops of wine from the bottle. "We should probably walk around the neighborhood tomorrow evening after dinner. That was about the same time I was making my delivery."

"And I'll see if I can reach Slade to set up a meeting," Marco said as he leaned down and gave me a kiss, slipping his hands around my waist. "Now, about our game plan for tonight."

I finished my wine in one gulp.

35

CHAPTER FOUR

Wednesday

I woke up to a newspaper headline that read:
MURDER VICTIM'S HUSBAND RELEASED.

I grabbed a cup of black coffee and dry toast and sat down at the table across from Marco to read the article, written by Connor MacKay.

According to a police spokesperson, the article began, Slade Rafferty, husband of murder victim Paige Rafferty, has been released from jail. The next line stopped me cold. "Oh, my God, Marco. Listen to this."

In a recent development, the DA's office has verified the claim that key evidence had been mishandled by officers arriving first on the scene. In an effort to reduce further jeopardizing the case, Chief of Police Samuel Baldwin has removed Sergeant Sean Reilly from active duty while an internal investigation can be completed.

At a press conference this morning, interim Sergeant Detective Richard Arno pleaded with the community. "Regardless of the unfortunate events surrounding this case, Slade Rafferty is still a main person of interest. We are calling on the citizens of New Chapel to come forward with any evidence you may have."

"Unfortunate events?" I crumpled the paper into a ball and threw it across the room. Our rescue cat Smoke, a beautiful Russian Blue, gave chase and continued batting it down the hallway toward our bedroom.

"Dutch is a liar, Marco, and this just confirmed it. He's lying to convict Rafferty and he's taking Reilly down, too."

"Woah, where's my Sunshine this morning? Reilly knew this was going to happen. That's why he hired us."

I tried to calm myself. Just thinking about Arno sent my nerves into overdrive. "You're right. We just have to solve this case before he does."

"There she is." Marco kissed me on the cheek just as our three-legged rescue mutt Seedy came galloping out of the bedroom with her three little paws clicking against the hardwood floor. She came to a quick stop at the sliding glass door as Smoke hopped over him and continued around her into the kitchen. "I'll take Seedy outside," Marco said, "and then we can start our morning workout."

I groaned, finished my coffee, and went to the sink looking around for Marco's coffee mug.

Just before sliding out of the back door, he said with a cheeky smile, "Check the dishwasher."

. . .

My staff was once again abuzz about the latest development in the case and it was almost nine before we finished discussing it. Lottie unlocked the front door and Rosa heeled her way to the work room, but Grace stopped suddenly before entering the tea parlor. She turned to look at me, "You know, love, something just occurred to me."

I slowly positioned the yellow smock around my head and tied the straps around my waist, feeling every aching muscle as I moved. "Tell me, Grace."

"I know Paige's sister, Susan. She and I are on the same bowling league. Quite a bowler, that one."

"Go on," I said.

"After a few drinks she's quite the talker as well," Grace continued. "Apparently, Paige was being harassed by her first husband ever since Susan had helped her get a divorce. I don't recall the man's name, but I do recall Susan's stories of abuse and they were quite disturbing. If there's someone you should be investigating, it's him."

I followed Grace into the parlor and watched as she retrieved a pen from behind the counter. "Do you think she would mind if Marco and I asked her a few questions?"

"Not at all. Her full name is Susan Gillen," Grace said, handing me a slip of paper. "I'll call her in advance and let her know why you want to talk to her. I know she'll be more than happy to help."

"Ask her if she'll see us this evening," I said, and headed off toward the workroom to check the orders for the day.

As soon as I parted the purple curtain and stepped into the room I felt my whole body relax. Although the space was windowless, the colorful blossoms and heady fragrances made the area feel like a tropical garden. Vases of all sizes and containers of dried flowers filled shelves above the counters along two walls. A large, slate-covered worktable occupied the middle of the room; two big walk-in coolers took up one side, and a desk holding my computer equipment and telephone filled the other side. Beneath the table were sacks of potting soil, green foam, and a plastic lined trash can.

I saw a stack of orders on the spindle waiting to be filled and more were coming in online. My cell phone rang and Marco's name popped up on the screen.

"Rafferty agreed to see us at his realty at twelve-fifteen today. I'll pick you up at noon."

"Fantastic. See you then."

I turned around, took a deep breath, and said, "Rosa, you take the orders on the spindle and I'll take the orders on our website. We need to work fast. I've got to be out of here at noon."

"We could always ask your cousin to help," Rosa said.

"Are you kidding?" I asked. "I made the mistake of telling Jill that I needed to lose some weight before the cruise and now she won't stop pestering me about it. That's a hard no, Rosa. We are *not* calling my cousin."

"No need to call," Rosa said as the purple curtain swung wide open.

Jillian flounced her way into the workroom and plopped her oversized Louis Vuitton Neverfull bag on the slab oak table. Her long, coppery red hair was pulled up in a pony-tail and she was dressed in a breezy patterned skirt with a matching light red tank top. "What does it take these days to get a text back from my one and only cousin?"

39

Before I could finish rolling my eyes, she pulled off her large oval sunglasses and continued.

"We have three weeks to get you in shape for this cruise, and by God, I will see this through to the end." She put her hands around one of my biceps. "Flex for me, Abs."

"Jillian, please. We have a lot of work to do."

"Oh, I know we do," she replied as she gently poked my belly. "And we'll start tonight. I'll be at your place at seven o'clock sharp. No need to confirm plans, considering you never respond to my texts, anyway. Oh, and you still have the yoga mat I gave you, right?"

"It's still in the trunk," I said.

"And the exercise ball?" she asked. "What about the fitness ring and the yoga block?"

"All in the trunk."

Jillian tried to stifle a giggle. "Seems as though you have a lot of junk in your trunk." She looked at Rosa for a confirmation laugh but upon receiving only a polite smile, continued, "Listen, Abs, I know you don't like exercising, but Pilatying is different."

Pilatying? I started to wonder if she had created the habit of mispronouncing words just so I would have a reason to respond. Instead of correcting her, I started my first order. An easy arrangement of red roses was first on the list so I headed toward the cooler.

Jillian was right behind me, still lecturing. "My whole life changed when I started Pilates," she said dramatically.

"Jill, you've been the same size since high school."

"It's not just weight control. It's about mind and body control, too."

40

I was my turn to stifle a laugh. My cousin, Jillian, a Harvard educated "kidult" who'd been spoiled by her parents because of severe scoliosis as a child, lecturing *me* about control. A year older than Jillian, a head shorter, and twenty pounds heavier, I'd always looked out for her so she wouldn't be bullied. As a result, she still depended on me way too much, even after surgery had corrected her spine and she blossomed into the most popular girl in our school.

Looking back, maybe I depended on her, too, to be the sister I never had. Perhaps I would give Pilates with Jillian a chance. What's the worst that could happen?

"Rosa," Jillian begged. "You're in good shape for your age. Please convince my stubborn cousin to work out with me."

"For my age?" Rosa responded. "How old do you think I am?"

Thoroughly caught off guard but never stumped, Jillian quickly changed the subject. "Do you know what they used to call Abby in high school?"

"Jill," I warned. "That's enough."

"It wasn't that she over ate or anything. She was just short and busty. High school kids are cruel, that's all. I used to defend her by reminding the other girls that they would kill to have such big –"

"That was a long time ago," I interrupted. "If I promise to exercise with you, will you leave us alone so we can work?"

"Only if you pinky swear," Jillian said with her hand outstretched, pinky extended.

I followed suit and Jillian lit up like a light bulb. "We are going to have so…much…fun!"

My eyes rolled full circle as Jillian scooped up her purse and looped it through her fit, tanned arm.

"Just think of it," Jillian said, "three weeks from today we will be sunbathing on the deck of a cruise ship, floating away to paradise, and I will be darned if anyone calls my cousin 'Flabby Abby' ever again. You have my word."

And with that, Jillian was out the curtain and announcing her goodbyes to my assistants.

Rosa didn't say a word. My old high school nickname hung in the air between us as the bell above the shop's door jingled and Jillian made her exit. Although I had come to terms with my height and stature as I had matured, the familiar rhyming ridicule still haunted me. It wasn't Jillian's intention to bring up old wounds, and I know she was only trying to help, but instead of motivating me to work harder it just made me sink deeper into myself.

Rosa set down her sheers and spun her finished arrangement so I could see. She met me by the spindle for her next order and nudged me. "I don't think you're flabby, mi chica."

"Thanks, Rosa," I said and began to place bright green cedar leaves between the roses. I stopped and inhaled the wonderfully fragrant mixture of scents. Nothing could calm me like the smell of flowers. I tied a white, laced ribbon around the bundle and wrapped the arrangement in green packaging paper.

"What do you think she meant by that?"

"By Flabby Abby? It's an old nickname. That's all."

"No, not that."

"Then what?" I asked.

"'Good shape for my age.'"

"Oh, that's just Jillian being Jillian," I said.

Rosa pulled a compact mirror from her purse and began fluffing her hair and sculpting her curves, muttering something under her breath in Spanish. It was amazing to me that someone so voluptuous and charismatic could have insecurities of her own. It made me feel better about myself, albeit selfishly, that I wasn't the only one.

"Don't pay any attention to her, Rosa. You are a beautiful, young woman. Now, let's get to work!"

And work we did. Rosa synched her phone to our mini-speaker system and we settled into our routine. Rosa and I had become quite the unstoppable team, especially when working to the upbeat tempos of her music.

By noon, I was out the door and hopping into Marco's car waiting at the curb, my stomach rumbling loudly as I closed the door. He must have noticed my immediate shock.

"What?" Marco asked.

"You know what," I said. "Where is it?"

"Not today, Sunshine."

"But you always bring me lunch," I said. "It's tradition! How am I going to concentrate on this interview when I have a hole growing in my stomach?"

"Here," Marco said as he pulled a protein bar from his console. "That's all I have."

"Down The Hatch has a full kitchen."

"We're already late," he replied. "Going one hour with food won't kill you."

I folded my arms and huffed as Marco pulled away from the curb. "Going an hour without food may not kill me, but you'd better watch your back."

Marco smiled and bit down into his mushy protein bar.

CHAPTER FIVE

"What's our strategy?" I asked.

"You start with your questions about the house and the mug and I'll pick it up from there."

"Deal."

Rafferty's realty, Executive Homes, was a short ten-minute drive across town. Slade greeted us warmly and asked us to have a seat in the two upholstered beige chairs that faced his modern teak wood desk. He was an average looking man with trimmed silver hair parted at the side. He was wearing a stylish grey suit, a thick silver watch and pearl-laced glasses, highlighting his brilliantly bright blue eyes.

He sat down in his beige, tweed executive's chair and leaned forward. "I appreciate you taking an interest in my wife's" -his breath seemed to catch in his throat. He composed himself then said, "I've read about you and your husband many times in the newspaper and I'm glad you've come to see me. May I ask who sent you?"

"As of right now, Mr. Rafferty," I answered. "We aren't at liberty to say."

Slade nodded and retrieved a pen from his desk, making a note as I continued.

"I don't know whether you're aware of this, but I was the first to arrive on the scene. I came to deliver your flowers, found the door open, and called the police, so I feel like I have a vested interest in your case."

"The flowers," he said fondly. "You were the one delivering the flowers. I had completely forgotten about that." He took a deep breath and said, "Paige loved flowers. She would spend hours out in her garden. She had just finished planting for the season." His eyes drifted away.

"I'm so sorry for your loss," I said, giving him a moment to collect himself.

"Thank you," he said.

"Would it be okay if we started with some personal questions?"

He hesitated for just a second then said, "Go ahead."

His brief hesitation was just long enough for me to feel a bit of distance between us. Marco shifted back in his seat, clearly feeling it, too.

I pulled out my iPad and took the lead. "First of all, are you able to get back into your house?"

"I will be tomorrow."

"That has to be a relief," I said.

"Yes and no," he replied. Considering what he was going home to, no further explanation was needed.

"Where were you on Monday at six p.m.?" I asked.

"Normally I would have been leaving work at six, but I received a phone call from a potential client asking me to take a look at a new home site. If I had said no" —his voice broke on the last word. He took a deep breath and said, "I waited for about thirty minutes, but the client never showed up at the property."

"Can this client vouch for your whereabouts?" I asked.

"That's where things get a little sticky," he answered. "This potential client said his name was Mr. Smith, but I have never met the man nor do I have any record of him in our system."

"Which means you have no alibi," I confirmed.

"My secretary relayed the phone call. She's my only alibi. We voluntarily offered to take lie detector tests, by the way, but Detective Arno said they weren't necessary. I'm meeting with my lawyers this afternoon and we are considering filing a lawsuit against him and the police department."

"Good for you," I said.

Marco nudged my knee with his. I wasn't supposed to take sides.

"Thinking back to Monday morning," I asked, "did you have coffee before you left for work?"

"Yes, at breakfast with my wife, as I do - did - every day." He stopped to look toward the window, pressing his lips into a hard line as though struggling to keep a professional face. I could tell by Marco's quick glance toward me that he seemed to be wavering on the sincerity of Slade's demeanor.

"Do you put your coffee cup in the dishwasher when you're finished?" I asked, drawing Slade's gaze back to me.

His eyes were watery but his composure was back. "No. It was Paige's habit to wash our dishes immediately and put them away."

I showed him the photo of the mug stand. "As you can see two cups are missing. One was still on the kitchen table beside your wife when the police arrived. I'm trying to account for the whereabouts of the second mug because I believe Paige was having coffee with someone before I got there. Do you know where Paige might have put the second mug?"

"I'm not sure."

I rephrased the question, "Could she have put the cup in the dishwasher?"

"Yes, possibly," he said.

"Would you check the dishwasher when you get back into your house and let me know what you find?" I asked. "If the mug is there, use a tissue or napkin to put it in a plastic bag and we'll come get it."

"Of course," he said and made a note.

"Again, going back to Monday," Marco added, "did your wife mention that she was expecting company, or is there anyone you can think of that might have dropped by to see her? A friend or a neighbor?"

"She didn't mention anything to me, but it's possible," Slade answered. "Our neighbor, Darlene Cutler, she comes by quite often and they may have been having coffee. She lives across the street from us."

I made a note as he relayed the address and highlighted the name Darlene Cutler.

"Did the detectives inform you that it appears someone set up your house to look like a break-in?"

"Detective Arno made it a point by accusing *me* of doing it," Slade replied bitterly, "killing my wife on our first anniversary no less. He said he had proof that I'd just gotten her to take out a huge life insurance policy."

"Did she?" Marco asked.

"If she did I was not aware," Slade replied. "I told Arno that I wanted proof and he quickly changed the subject."

I gritted my teeth. That sounded like the way Dutch worked. He would lie to convict his own grandmother if it would close a case. I quickly typed *insurance policy* as Slade continued.

"Then I asked for my lawyer and that ended the questions."

"Have you checked your wife's account to see if her charge cards were used?" Marco asked.

"Yes. It's a joint account, by the way, and nothing has been charged on it since Sunday when I took her to Chicago to buy her an anniversary gift."

He looked toward the window, his thoughts spinning off as he said wistfully, "She picked out a diamond watch and a crystal cell phone case from Nordstrom's." This time he swiveled his chair completely away and buried his face in his hands, his shoulders shaking in silent sobs.

I leaned close to Marco to whisper, "I think we've put him through enough for one session."

"Not yet, Abby. Trust me on this."

"Then let's give him a minute. He's doing all he can to keep his composure."

At Marco's nod, I busied myself by pulling out my phone to check messages.

The first was from Jillian: *Pilates. Tonight. 7pm.*

The other was from Grace: *Paige's sister will be home this evening if you want to talk to her. You have her number. She'll be expecting your call.*

I showed Grace's text to Marco and he gave me a thumbs-up. Things were moving quickly, thank goodness, but not quickly enough for my stomach. It growled loudly and I glowered at my husband.

After a few moments, Slade used a tissue to wipe his nose then turned back to us. "I'm sorry. I'm still in a state of shock. Nothing about this makes sense to me."

"Were you told that your wife's ring is missing?" Marco asked, jumping right back in.

"Yes," Slade said.

"Does she always wear her ring?" I asked.

"Always, even when she's gardening. She never takes it off. Excuse me. She never *took* it off."

"Do you have a photo of the ring, a close up if possible?"

"The detectives confiscated my cell phone," he said, "but I can pull up a photo online and show it to you." Just as he had turned to his desk computer, Slade's office phone rang, which seemed to startle him. He quickly punched a button that hung up the call automatically.

I pulled out my phone and snapped photos as Slade scrolled through engagement photos on his computer. The main diamond was extravagant, with two smaller diamonds on either side.

Marco continued his questioning, "Does anyone besides you and your wife have a key to your house?"

"Only two people -- Paige's sister, Susan, and Darlene Cutler. Susan had a spare for emergencies and Darlene always watered our plants when we went down to our Florida home in the winter."

"How long has Darlene had a key?" Marco asked.

"Since we bought our place five years ago," Slade replied. "Why?"

"We think someone got into the house either without alarming your wife or without your wife knowing," Marco said. "Do you have any reason to suspect Darlene Cutler would want to hurt Paige?"

"Not at all," Slade replied easily. "They were very close. Paige would bring over vegetables from the garden and Darlene would bring cakes and pies. She was a good neighbor, except..." he trailed off for a moment.

"Except what, Mr. Rafferty?" Marco asked.

"Darlene's son," he continued. "He was trouble."

"What's his name?" I asked.

"Dylan," Slade said and then made another note before looking back up at us. "Dylan Cutler had been living with his mom when we first moved into our home. The police would be at their house quite often and there were break-ins all over the neighborhood. He was arrested for drug possession soon after we moved in."

"How does that pertain to this case?" Marco asked.

"Dylan was released from prison last month," Slade said, his eyes were looking in our direction but his focus was far away. "That's when the break-ins started happening again. Paige would give him odd jobs around the house to help him out. I told her I didn't trust the kid, but Paige was so kind." He looked toward the window, his thoughts spinning off again as he said to himself, "I told her not to help him."

50

"Do you believe Dylan Cutler could have located the key his mother kept for your house and used it to gain entry?" Marco asked.

"I'm sure he could have."

"And do you believe Dylan would have had coffee with Paige and then stage a robbery?"

"He was a drug addict," Slade bellowed, his fists balling up on his desk. "I'm sure he was capable of anything."

Dylan Cutler was now number one on my suspects list, but Marco seemed to have a different idea. "Can you think of anyone else who might've wanted to hurt your wife?"

Slade stood up and walked around, rubbing his forehead. "Why would anyone want to hurt Paige?" he asked. "She was the kindest woman I have ever met, not an enemy in the world. She helped out everyone in need, couldn't say no to anyone." With that thought, Slade stopped pacing. He turned and said, "Luke Hurst."

I quickly jumped back to my iPad as he continued.

"Luke is Paige's ex-husband. About six months after we were married, he started calling and texting her about being fired, playing on her sympathies to get loans from her, which of course were never paid back. After I overheard one of his calls, Paige finally admitted she'd been helping him, so I told her to stop before his demands escalated.

"Things were quiet until about two months ago when he started harassing her with text messages, begging her for more money and threatening to kill himself. I asked Paige to save the texts and then had her file a restraining order against him. The texts will be on Paige's phone if it's ever located."

"Did you tell the detectives about Luke?" Marco asked.

"No," Slade replied. "Everything happened so fast. But I will now."

After making another note, Slade continued. "In all honesty, I don't have a good alibi and Arno knows it. He wanted a confession from me, not a theory on who actually might have wanted to harm Paige. Thank goodness my lawyer was able to get there quickly and put an end to Arno's bully tactics."

Those were my thoughts exactly, but my anger was momentarily overwhelmed by my rumbling stomach. I nudged Marco and then glanced at my watch to let him know I had to get back to the shop before my lunch hour was over. He gave me a nod back.

"Is there anything else you can tell us about Luke Hurst?" Marco asked. "Where he lives? Where he's working now?"

Slade shook his head. "Once the calls and texts stopped, Paige and I didn't talk about Luke anymore."

Marco and I rose. "Thank you for your time," Marco said, shaking his hand. He gave Slade a business card. "If you think of anything else, please call."

"You never told me who you were working for," Slade said as we were leaving.

Marco and I both paused and looked at him, his demeanor strikingly different from just seconds earlier. "You've already asked my wife that, Mr. Rafferty," Marco said politely. "We are not at liberty to say."

"I see. I see," Slade said. "Oh, Abby. I almost forgot to ask, when I ordered the tulip arrangement, I gave Grace an anniversary card to put in the box. Do you know what happened to it?"

"I still have the arrangement," I told him.

He heaved a sigh of relief. "Inside the card you'll find two cruise tickets. I'll need those returned, please."

"I'll get it to you right away," I said. "And don't forget to check for that mug."

CHAPTER SIX

As we headed for Marco's silver Prius, I asked, "Was it just me, or was there something odd about Slade Rafferty?"

"He was questioned by the detectives and failed to mention a drug addict neighbor and harassing ex-husband," Marco said. "That seems very odd to me."

"It's more than that," I said. "Something about him just seemed off. Hanging up on that incoming call, and taking notes while we interviewed him, what do you think that was about?"

"I caught a glance when we stood up," Marco said as we stopped at his car, "and it was exactly that."

"What?"

"Notes," he said. "Slade was taking notes about the interview just like you were. I've interviewed many people, but I've never had someone take notes."

"Very strange," I said, "but I still don't think he's the killer."

"Based on?"

"He had flowers delivered to his house at the same time Paige was killed," I began. "If Slade had planned to kill his wife and stage a robbery, then why invite a potential witness to the crime in progress?"

"That's a very good point," Marco said, squeezing my hand. "I hadn't thought of that."

"Plus, there was that whole Mr. Smith ploy to make sure Slade wasn't at home at the time of the murder."

"It could be a ploy," Marco said, "or it could be Slade's cover story. He could easily have called his own secretary and told her to put that appointment on his calendar to set up an alibi, albeit a very slim one, but enough to throw the detectives off his trail, especially when there are two very likely suspects waiting in the wings."

"I highly doubt that, Marco."

"Yes, but don't discount it either. If Slade had planned to kill his wife and stage a robbery, any good detective would be all over Dylan Cutler and Luke Hurst. Perhaps Slade was counting on competent detective work and wound up caught in his own trap. Maybe for once Arno is right."

"I hope you're not serious," I said.

"I'm just playing—"

"I know what you're playing, but there are more sinister devil's that you could advocate, like Dylan Cutler, just released from prison, a drug addict. What about him?"

"From what Slade told us, the motive for Dylan would be money, but we have no verification."

"And ex-husband, Luke Hurst?"

"Luke is someone I wouldn't mind talking to. From what we know, his motive would also be money, but with ex-husbands the motive is usually much deeper." He added, "If we could get a look at those texts that Luke sent to Paige, we would have some much needed verification."

"Her phone is still missing," I said. "Do you have the ability to track it?"

"I don't, but maybe Reilly does."

"That would be risky," I thought aloud. "Wouldn't the detective already be tracking it?"

"Good detectives would," he answered. "I'll talk to Reilly and see what he thinks. In the meantime, we have plenty of people to interview."

Marco opened the passenger door for me, but I stayed for a moment and couldn't help but think about Slade Rafferty actually murdering his own wife. It just didn't seem right. Nothing about this case seemed right. "Marco, would you buy me extravagant jewelry, pay for an expensive cruise, and then kill me?"

He thought about it for a moment then answered, "That depends."

"On what?"

"On whether I wanted to look innocent or not."

"So you've thought about this, have you?" I asked playfully.

Marco put his arms around me and pulled me in for a hug. "Of course not, Sunshine," he said and kissed me on the cheek. "I could find a much cheaper way to look innocent."

I gave him a jab in the ribs. "I'm being serious."

"So am I," he said, laughing. "It could be a ploy to look innocent. Now why don't you call Paige's sister and set up an interview for after supper? She might be able to shed light on both Luke's and Slade's relationship with Paige."

I pulled out my cell phone. "I'm on it now."

As soon as I was back at Bloomers, Grace and I found the anniversary card with the cruise tickets in it. The shop was quiet and the orders were complete so we spent the rest of the day talking about Paige's murder. We discussed the interview with Slade and everyone seemed to agree that it would be odd to send flowers to your own house while you were committing a premeditated murder. Although we agreed on most details, the ladies were still very torn about the guilt of Slade Rafferty.

I left Bloomers around four and headed back to Slade Rafferty's realty office to return the cruise tickets, noticing that he and Paige would have been travelling on the same boat as us. On the way, I called Dylan's mom, Darlene Cutler, and set up a quick meeting with her at Rosie's diner the next morning. Rafferty's realty building was quiet as I entered the lobby and approached Slade's office door.

"You can leave them with me," his secretary said, coming around the corner with a steaming cup of tea. "Mr. Rafferty isn't in at the moment."

"Do you know when he might be back?" I asked.

"Honestly, I don't know," she said with slight concern in her voice. "He left around one for a meeting with his lawyers and hasn't returned."

"Is that normal?"

"Not really," she said and then stopped herself. "I'm sorry, Abby. I don't mean to trouble you. I'll give him the tickets and let him know you stopped by."

I got home around five and was greeted warmly by my sweet, three-legged mutt, Seedy. From around the corner casually strolled Smoke, our giant Russian Blue rescue cat. He let out a curt meow and headed straight for his food dish.

"I know, Smokey boy. I'm hungry, too."

After feeding our pets and taking Seedy out for a quick walk I was caught standing in front of the open refrigerator.

"Guess what's for dinner?" Marco asked as he kicked off his shoes and came up behind me for a kiss.

"Meatloaf? Mashed potatoes? Oven-roasted ham…"

"Salad it is," he said enthusiastically, revealing a large takeout container from Down The Hatch.

"How am I going to live through three weeks of this?"

"You can do it, babe."

Right. "By the way, I stopped by Rafferty's realty office after work."

"And?"

"Rafferty wasn't there. His secretary said he left for his meeting at one and never came back."

Marco reached around me and grabbed the Italian vinaigrette from the side panel, then shut the refrigerator door. "Is that significant?"

"I'm not sure, but his secretary seemed to think so. I just wanted you to know."

"Did you get in touch with Darlene Cutler?"

"Yes, and that's Doctor Cutler. She's a child psychologist. The only time she could meet with us is tomorrow morning at 9 am."

"Well," Marco said. "That's extremely inconvenient."

"Apparently," I said as I prepared my air quotes. "She's a 'very busy woman.' But I can get one of my assistants to cover for me."

"Then let's do it."

We ate our healthy dinner and talked over the case, laying out different strategies and theories. I popped the last cherry tomato into my mouth and sank in, savoring every last bite.

"That salad wasn't so bad," I said. "And I am surprisingly full. Good job, hubby."

"Being on a diet takes some getting used to," he replied, "but I'm glad you liked it." Marco picked up one of the glasses of Chardonnay that I'd poured, and I picked up the other. "Here's to saving our friend Sean Reilly," he said, clinking glasses with me.

"And here's to showing Dutch how to solve a case the right way," I said, and we clinked again.

We were almost on our way to canvass the Rafferty's neighborhood when my phone dinged to signal an incoming text. It was from Jillian: *On my way!*

"Oh, shoot," I said and grabbed Marco's sleeve, stopping him before he opened the door to the garage.

I texted back: *I am soooo sorry, Jill. I completely forgot. Busy with the case.*

"What's wrong?" Marco asked.

"I told Jillian I would do Pilates with her tonight. I totally spaced it." *Possibly on purpose.*

"She's not going to be happy about that," Marco teased.

"I think she'll understand."

Jillian replied: *BUT YOU PINKY SWORE!*

"Okay, maybe not," I said to Marco.

My reply was short but sincere: *So sorry. Tomorrow. 7 pm. I promise.*

Her response was a sad face emoji.

...

We canvassed the residents of Sandy Creek Court but came up with no new information. Some of the neighbors had seen the police cars, and some had even noticed my Bloomers van, but no one had noticed any strange cars in the alley, or seen anyone at Paige's front door, or even heard the sound of a window being smashed. Whoever had entered the Rafferty's home had gotten in without being spotted.

At eight-thirty that evening, I rang the doorbell at the home of Susan Gillen. A divorced woman who worked as a branch manager for New Chapel Savings Bank, the attractive forty-six-year old divorcee lived in a one-bedroom condominium in a beautiful new complex near the university.

I was instantly overwhelmed by the distinct and nauseating aroma of ammonia mixed with something else equally unbearable. I almost took a step back, but was ushered inside.

"Quickly now," she said, "step inside. We don't want anyone escaping, do we?"

And then I realized that she wasn't just talking to me and Marco, but instead to a room full of darting, furry animals.

"Don't mind the smell," she said.

"It's okay," I tried to say between breaths through my mouth. "I can hardly smell the litterbox."

"The litterbox? Oh, no. Those are in the basement. I meant about the fishy smell. I made tuna for dinner."

"We have a cat too," I said, looking around at the feline décor and paintings. "He eats everything, but for the life of me I can't get him to eat tuna."

"Oh, no," she corrected again. "The tuna was for me."

"I see."

Marco gave me a look of frightful desperation.

"Let's get straight to the questions, shall we?"

Susan poured chamomile tea into cups and handed them to us before taking a seat on a blue chair across from where we were seated on the couch. A large orange tabby leapt onto my lap with a frisky meow and I was compelled to pet him with one hand while I opened my iPad with the other.

"First of all, I need to ask if you stopped by Paige's house on Monday to have coffee with her," Marco said, as I balanced the cat on my knees.

"No, I was out of town until Monday evening," she said.

I made notes while Marco continued and the tabby rubbed his nose on my chin.

"Tell us about Slade and Paige's marriage."

A gray and white tiger cat jumped onto the sofa and curled up beside her. She instinctively caressed him while she answered, "Slade was wonderful to my sister. He treated Paige as a beautiful, independent woman, not as a possession, like Luke had."

"Do you know anything about Slade taking out a life insurance policy on Paige?" I asked.

"Oh, no," she denied. "I handle all of their personal finances and I haven't seen anything unusual."

"What are your feelings about Slade being your sister's killer?" Marco asked, getting right to the point.

"I don't believe it for a second. He adored Paige as much as she adored him. In fact, she told me only last week-" Susan gulped back tears and started over, her voice breaking. "She told me – only last week – that she'd never – felt as loved as when –"

She covered her face and began to sob so hard she had to leave the room. The cat, startled, jumped down and trotted after her. I knew exactly how Paige had felt about her husband because I'd gone through a similar life-changing event.

I'd been engaged to the eldest son of one of the scions of New Chapel, Pryce Osborne II, but I'd never felt he'd truly loved me. He'd just wanted someone his family deemed worthy of being his wife, and once I'd flunked out of law school, I'd flunked out as his fiancée too, a stain on their high social standing in the community. It was only under Marco's love that I'd blossomed.

Sensing my thoughts, Marco gave my hand a squeeze and gazed into my eyes, his reflecting that same deep love I felt for him. I gave him a grateful smile and he said, "We need to get out of here. My eyes are burning."

Susan came back into the living room, a different cat in her arms, composed once again. "I'm so sorry," she said in a voice still constricted with pain. "My sister and I were very close. Losing her has been the worst thing I've ever endured."

"And I'm sorry to have to put you through this," I said, "but we believe the detectives aren't looking at all the evidence."

"You better believe they're not," Susan said angrily. "They're ignoring everything I told them. I informed Detective Arno what Luke Hurst had been doing to my sister and that he should be investigated, too, not just Slade. He listened with obvious disinterest, didn't take any notes, and thanked me curtly. So I took it upon myself to call Luke and ask him where he was on Monday afternoon. He merely hung up on me."

"Slade told us what he knew about Luke asking Paige for money," I said. "What can you tell us about that?"

"I can tell you that Slade didn't know everything. Paige didn't like to upset him. In fact, she knew neither one of us liked her helping Luke out, but that was my kind-hearted sister. She had a hard time refusing anyone. She always wanted to believe the best in everyone."

"Slade told us that Paige had filed a restraining order against Luke," I said. "Do you know if Paige had any contact with him since then?"

"Yes, a few weeks ago I happened to be at the house when Luke called. He told her he was out of work again, looking for a new job, and, as usual, wasn't able to pay his rent. She asked me not to mention it to Slade because he'd just get angry. I told her he had every right to

63

be angry. She was being a fool, and if she couldn't say no to Luke, then for heaven's sake, stop answering his calls!"

Susan huffed, clearly still upset, and reached for her tea, giving me a chance to catch up on my notes before continuing.

"At my urging," she said, "Paige finally called Luke back to tell him she'd changed her mind about lending the money. And then she did exactly what I'd advised her to do, stopped taking his calls. That was when he started sending her emails."

"Slade must not have known about the emails," I said to Marco.

"I doubt he knew," Susan said. "She confided that to me."

"And those emails could be why the computer is missing," I said to Marco. "I'm sorry for interrupting again, Susan. Go on."

"Actually, you're right, Abby," Susan said. "Luke wouldn't have wanted those emails discovered. Anyway, Paige blocked his email address, and then he started texting her so she blocked his number, too. He didn't pay any attention to that restraining order."

"Theoretically, Luke was blocked on all fronts except one," I said, "to show up at her house and ask for the money in person."

"That's very possible," Susan said. "He could've easily talked his way inside."

"Given all that harassment, would she have felt comfortable enough to have had coffee with him?" Marco asked.

"If he asked for a cup, I'm sure she would have. Take it from me. Luke could be very humble and convincing when he wanted something." Through gritted

64

teeth she said, "I'll never forgive him for the way he treated my sister. If he's the one who killed her, I hope he rots in prison."

"We're going to do everything we can to find your sister's killer," I assured her.

"Would you please keep me informed? I can't get Detective Arno to return my calls."

"Of course." I dug one of our cards out of my purse. "Thank you so much for seeing us, Susan. If you think of anything else that might help, please call. Oh, and one more thing. Do you have Luke's address?"

"No, but I know where he always used to hang out. It's a pool hall and bar on the south side of town, just off Route Thirty, called The Lost Weekend."

"I know the one you mean," Marco said. "Thanks."

We walked back to the Prius, taking turns swiping cat fur from each other's clothing. Marco's phone rang as we got into the car, "It's Reilly," he said and put the phone on speaker. "How's desk life, Reilly?"

"Don't get me started. I feel like a zoo animal," he said quietly. "Everyone in the precinct is watching me, waiting to see what I do next. It's humiliating."

"I'm sorry, Sarge," I said into the speaker. Marco moved the phone closer to me. "It's Abby. Do you have any news for us?"

"I just got an email from our tech specialist," Reilly started. "He can track the phone without a warrant, but he's nervous about taking orders from me now that I'm being investigated. He didn't promise anything, so we'll see. He said that if the phone is powered on he can locate the wireless signal pretty accurately, but there's the problem."

"The phone's not on," I said.

"Probably not," Reilly confirmed. "Most likely the phone was either destroyed or powered off. The good news is that the phone can be tracked up until that point, so we may have something within a day or two. He said he would get back to me if he could."

"Thank you, Sean," Marco said. "Just let us know."

"Will do," Reilly said before hanging up.

It wasn't until we were almost home that Marco asked, "What are you thinking?"

"That we have a new top suspect — Luke Hurst"

CHAPTER SEVEN

Thursday

I rolled over to find my husband sitting up in bed reading the newspaper. "Good morning," I squeaked, then cleared my throat. "How long have you been up?"

"Long enough to take Seedy out and grab the paper," he replied without looking at me. "Get this, Slade Rafferty was picked up last night by NCPD for drunk and disorderly conduct across the street from his home. I wonder if he paid a visit to Dylan Cutler?"

"Oh my God. What else does it say?"

"Not much, other than that he's being held at the jail for further questioning."

"Wow. What was he thinking?"

"You said he didn't return to work yesterday," Marco said, "and we saw him taking notes during our interview." He looked at me. "Maybe Slade knows something we don't."

"We're going to see Darlene Cutler this morning. Maybe she can fill us in."

Marco put down the paper. "Actually, *you're* going to see Darlene Cutler. I woke up to a text from Rafe. He can't open the bar, claiming he has the flu."

"No Rosie's breakfast for you!" I looked at the clock and shot out of bed. "I'm going to get there a little early. I could really go for a fried egg sandwich, and some bacon and hash browns…"

"Every bite you eat is another five minutes at Marco's gym. Don't forget."

I poked my head out of the closet and gave my husband the death glare but he didn't flinch. "Fine," I answered dryly. "Grapefruit and toast."

"I'll have to trust you on that," he said.

"After breakfast I'm going to make an appointment to see Greg Morgan and tell him what's going on, see what he says about Arno's behavior."

"Just be careful you don't get Reilly in more trouble, Sunshine. He's in a precarious position right now."

"Don't worry. I know how to handle Morgan. Are we still planning on paying a visit to the Lost Weekend pool hall this evening?"

"You bet. We need to keep this case rolling."

...

Rosie's Diner, one block west of the town square, was the hotspot in town for breakfast, so I wasn't surprised to see the tables full. The diner had the traditional booths around the perimeter and tables in the center, with a lunch counter along the back wall. Rosie herself still waited on customers at the counter and rang up the tabs, so I stopped by to say hello.

"Hey, kiddo," Rosie said with a smile. "Haven't seen you around in a while. How've you been?"

"Busy with the flower shop and helping Marco with his private eye work. I see it's as hopping in here as ever."

"You know it," she said with a wink, "but your table's ready and your party's already arrived." Rosie nodded toward one of the booths by the window. Seated with her back to us, reading a newspaper, was Darlene Cutler. She had long, dark, straightened hair, wearing a dark grey blazer and matching knee-length skirt. One long leg was crossed demurely over the other, her heel sticking out, tapping rhythmically.

"Hello," I said as I scooted into the booth across from her. "I'm Abby Knight Salvare."

She lowered the paper and pulled the dark-rimmed glasses down on her nose. Her face was thin and pointy, but her cheeks were supple and jawline carved. Her eyes were brown, trimmed with long, black lashes, her makeup was thick but professional. She was quite stunning, even through her dark business attire I could tell she was fit and took care of herself. I was immediately jealous.

After giving me the quick once-over she removed her glasses and extended her hand. "It's a pleasure to meet you, Abby. I'm sure you've seen the paper this morning." She folded up the newspaper and set it next to her purse by her side. "There should be no doubt, now, as to the true nature of Slade Rafferty, but I am glad you asked to see me."

"And why do you say that, Dr. Cutler?"

"You can call me Darlene," she said pleasantly.

The waitress halted at our table with a large tray and set it down next to me. My stomach growled at the aroma, like an attack dog warding off an intruder. I glanced at the tray filled with plates of eggs and sausage, biscuits and gravy, pancakes, buttered toast and finally, bacon. Then I watched as the waitress off-loaded several plates onto our table, placing the stack of pancakes right under my nose.

"I'm sorry," I said, trying not to drool. "I haven't ordered yet."

"No," Darlene corrected. "Those are for me. And I'll need a fresh jar of syrup. This one's sticky."

"All of this is for you?" I asked as the waitress began clearing room for more plates of greasy, buttery, fried —

"You know," Darlene said. "I have the metabolism of a teenager. I can eat and eat. Feel free to share. I never finish it all."

I swallowed hard as the waitress stood ready to take my order. My lips were dry as I heard the words come out of my mouth. "Grapefruit and toast, please."

The waitress left and I watched Darlene Cutler rub white, fluffy butter onto her pancakes. My stomach gave me a hard nudge, almost caving to the offer, but I fought the urge as she continued talking. "I don't know how anyone survives on grapefruit and toast. I would curl up in a ball and die if that's all I ate."

Tell me about it.

"Darlene, I have a few questions, if you don't mind."

"Naturally," she said after finishing her first bite, "and I have answers. Go ahead."

"First, tell me about last night."

"Okay, I was in my study, catching up on some work, and heard a loud pounding at my door. Between Dylan, the police, and now, this whole murder investigation, it takes a lot to startle me, but this was different."

She took a bite of her eggs and I took a long drink of my ice-cold tap water before she continued. "I could hear Slade calling out for Dylan. He shattered a coffee cup against my front door, raving like a madman, so I called the police."

A coffee cup. There goes the evidence. "Was Dylan at home?"

She didn't answer right away. The waitress came with her syrup and my pathetic breakfast. Darlene oozed the syrup over her pancakes and I was momentarily hypnotized by the fluid moving over the stack. "No, he was not."

"Who was what?"

"Dylan was not at home," she repeated. "I'm going to tell you something about my son and I don't want you to get the wrong idea, but before I do I want to let you know that Slade Rafferty is not the man everyone thinks he is."

"Why do you say that?"

"I'm a psychologist," she began. "I specialize in child psychology, but the majority of the training is the same as that of an adult. Slade Rafferty exhibits all of the behaviors of someone having possessive personality disorder."

I made a mental note as she continued talking – and eating.

"I knew Paige very well. She was the realtor who sold me my home, and after that, became a dear friend. Shortly after marrying Slade, she was no longer allowed to work, relegated instead to taking care of the home and garden."

"Do you think he killed her?"

"I can't say for certain, but I can tell you that Slade was very possessive of her. My son would come to the house and help out with odd jobs, but Paige was very insistent that her husband never find out."

"Did you visit Paige the day of the murder?"

"I have a very busy practice," she answered indirectly. "I work long hours."

"So you didn't stop by for coffee around six?"

"No, I returned home much later that evening."

I poked at my grapefruit while Darlene crunched down on a slice of bacon. "Tell me about Dylan," I said.

"Well," she replied, but hesitantly, finishing her bite and giving me a long look before continuing. "I'm sure you've discovered by now that Dylan has always been a troubled boy. I blame his father, and, of course, his father blames me. We divorced when Dylan was very young. His father couldn't handle the fact that I was intelligent and successful, and apparently, Dylan couldn't handle it either."

Modest.

"He's never listened to me. He stayed with his father throughout high school and then with me when the money ran dry. I paid for his college, and upon dropping out of that, paid for his technical training as well. Unfortunately, the drugs took control long before I could and I had to give up on the boy."

"How could you give up on your son?"

"There's only so much you can take before you realize that giving up is the only way to stay sane. After the drugs took over, he was no longer my son. I thought maybe prison would straighten him out, but it's only made things worse."

"Was Dylan at the Rafferty's home on Monday evening?" I asked. "Do you think he has anything to do with Paige's murder?"

"I can't account for my son's whereabouts anymore, and I don't want to think about what he's capable of now."

"Then why do you let him stay with you?"

She put her fork down and looked at me with deep sincerity. A single tear formed under her eye and she blinked it away. "Just because I've given up on my son doesn't mean that I'm not still his mother."

"You're right. I'm sorry."

"I've spent my whole career helping children in need. I guess mine is the ultimate story of irony, wouldn't you say, unable to help the only child who truly matters to me?"

Just then Darlene's phone rang inside her purse. She grabbed the phone and excused herself. I made a few notes on my phone and then poked again at the grapefruit with my fork. After one bite I gave up and devoured the dry toast.

"I'm sorry," Darlene said, returning to the table. "Something's come up and I've got to go."

"I just have a few more questions," I pleaded. "It won't take long."

"Hurry please," she said as she dug in her purse for her wallet.

"Do you know who Luke Hurst is?"

"No," she answered. "I don't believe I've ever heard that name."

I quickly described Luke's appearance and his connection to the investigation.

"I'm sorry," she said and shook her head. "I've never seen him."

"Do you still have the key to Paige's house?"

Darlene paused and looked up at me. "I'm sure I do. Why do you ask?"

"It's very important that you find the key."

"I know what you're getting at, Abby, but I don't think it matters anymore. I've just been notified that Dylan has been arrested in connection with Paige's murder. I've got to go speak with our attorney."

"Wait," I said before she could leave. "With what evidence?"

"He was caught with Paige's computer and wedding ring."

CHAPTER EIGHT

I sat at the table, staring at Darlene's untouched biscuits and gravy, before snapping myself out of it. Dylan Cutler had been caught with Paige's stolen items. From the evidence Marco and I had gathered that meant only one thing, Dylan Cutler had murdered Paige Rafferty. A few thoughts raced through my mind: Sergeant Reilly would be off the hook for interfering with a police investigation, Slade Rafferty was correct in assuming Dylan was connected, and I might have to actually do Pilates with Jillian tonight.

I finished my water, paid my bill, then rang up the Prosecutor's office. As usual, their secretary, Kirby, answered, a nasally voiced woman about my age who wore purple granny glasses and always pretended she didn't know who I was.

"Abby Knight Salvare," I repeated slowly, "and I want to make an appointment to meet with Greg as soon as possible."

"Mr. Morgan has a full schedule today. Let me see when I can fit you in."

"All I need is ten minutes of his time."

She put me on hold then came back moments later. "It looks like he'll be able to see you next Thursday at two o'clock."

"*Next* Thursday?"

"I'm afraid so."

I wasn't buying it. I thanked her and hung up without making the appointment. I'd just have to ambush Morgan. And I knew exactly when to do it. I looked at my watch. I didn't have much time.

I saw Greg talking to his boss Melvin Darnell on their way to the courthouse, a large, tall building, smack-dap in the middle of the square. The courthouse was built in the early nineteen hundreds and the weathered gray bricks had long since shown their age. The lawn around the building was well-maintained, with wide paths intersecting the square, and benches for people to sit and enjoy the atmosphere. I jogged across the street and hurried across the wide lawn, catching Morgan just before he got to the courthouse steps.

"Hey, Greg," I said breathlessly, holding my side, "can I have a few minutes of your time?"

"It's going to take you a few minutes to catch your breath, Abby. I don't have that much time."

My face was flush, which hid the red warning signs of anger spreading across my cheeks. "Don't start with me, Morgan."

He brushed a sweaty strand of my hair from my face. "I haven't even begun."

Gregory F. Morgan had been hired by the prosecutor's office straight out of law school, not because of his outstanding grades or academic achievements, I was certain, but because of his charming ways, good looks, and modicum of intelligence. He'd been the courthouse staff's golden boy ever since. He wasn't tall but he had a toned body that looked great in either a suit or jeans, chestnut colored hair with blond glints women would kill for, blue eyes that made you swear he'd stashed a halo somewhere, and a flawless smile that smacked of braces.

I'd had a crush on Greg in high school but he'd never noticed me then. It wasn't until I'd returned home from college with a fully developed figure that he'd suddenly started paying attention to me.

"You do know that Dylan Cutler has just been picked up in connection to the Paige Rafferty case, right?"

"When did this happen?" Greg asked.

"Just now, I think."

"Then how would I know?"

I shrugged. "But you do know what this means, right?"

This time he shrugged. "What are you getting at, Abby?"

"Here's the situation. A sergeant and his men discover a murder scene, begin investigating, and are then pulled off the case when a certain detective decides he wants to handle the case alone. Said sergeant mentions this to his captain, who speaks with a certain detective, and

77

suddenly said sergeant is put on desk duty and then accused of leaking information to the press with the threat of being given administrative leave."

"Okay, you can stop with the *said sergeant* stuff. I know who you're talking about." He continued up the short cement stairs as I followed.

"Great. Then you can understand my concern because you know damn well that Sean Reilly is a good officer and a good friend. Maybe what you don't know is that he *didn't* leak information to the press. That's a bogus charge. And I'd be happy to testify to that in a court of law because I was there with Connor Mackay when he eavesdropped on what Reilly and his officers were discussing.

"Calm yourself," Morgan said with a condescending charm. He reached out to brush away another strand and I swatted his hand.

"What I don't understand is why Arno took the actions he did. Why is he purposely trying to damage Reilly's career, because you know as well as I do what administrative leave means."

Morgan scratched his chin, thinking, so I blew the strand of hair from my eye and continued. "If Dylan is charged with the murder of Paige Rafferty then Sergeant Reilly should be allowed back to work. Arno has it out for him, and I want these accusations dropped immediately."

"Abby, I highly doubt that Detective Arno has it out for him. But you're right about his accusations against Sgt. Reilly. That shouldn't be happening without documented proof. Let me talk to my boss and see what he says. I'll get back to you as soon as I know something."

"Like next Thursday?"

He gave me a knowing scowl and opened the courthouse door. "As soon as I know something."

"Thanks, Greg," I said as he let the door close between us. "I appreciate it." I turned and swiftly headed back across the courthouse lawn. I couldn't wait to tell my staff about the new turn of events. I pulled out my phone to call Marco on my way to Bloomers but noticed he was already calling me.

"We have a problem," Marco said softly.

"What's wrong?"

"I think you better come to the bar."

"I'll be right there."

I entered Down The Hatch and saw Marco standing behind the bar. The light coming in from outside was dimmed by the darkened windows and the music was low. As always, the outdated décor jumped out at me. I had spent our entire courtship begging Marco to renovate, but he insisted that his customers liked it that way. He believed the fisherman's net hanging above the bar and the old, rustic paintings gave the bar its charm. I disagreed.

It was just before the lunch rush, so there were only a few people sitting at the tables. I made my way to Marco and saw Sean Reilly with his back to me, the lapel of his overcoat pulled up around his neck. I took the stool next to him. "What's wrong?"

Marco looked at me and then at Sean, encouraging him to speak first, but he didn't. Instead, Sean swiveled slightly in his seat and looked around at the bar. He had a dark mask of stubble around his chin and bags under his eyes. I had never seen him looking so rough. Marco reached down behind the bar and turned the music up just enough so that we wouldn't be overheard.

Finally, Reilly spoke. "The captain pulled me into his office last night and asked me to turn in my gun and badge."

"Oh, no," I said, my hand shooting up to cover my mouth in shock. "What does that mean?"

Reilly laughed, almost as if to hold back tears, and shrugged. "It means I'm done. I've been placed on leave. We failed."

"But Dylan was just picked up this morning in connection with Paige's murder," I explained. "If he's charged, then you should be in the clear."

"It's far beyond that now," Reilly said. He stared down at the empty bar, wringing his hands and shaking his head. "My email was monitored. They know about my communication with the tech specialist and my involvement with you and Marco."

"We think Slade Rafferty told Detective Arno about our investigation," Marco elaborated. "He must have tied us to Reilly. After Slade was picked up at the Cutler's house, Arno was seen investigating him again, and right after that he was cleared of all charges."

"Why would Arno do that?" I asked, then took a deep breath and reminded myself to talk softly again. "Why would he clear his number one suspect before Dylan was even arrested?"

"Rafferty must have told him something," Marco posited. "Maybe he knows something we don't."

"Darlene said that Slade threw a coffee cup at her front door while he was raving about Dylan," I said. "So that piece of evidence is out."

"It's not just about solving the case anymore," Reilly said solemnly. "This is personal now. Arno has wanted me gone for a long time."

Marco poured two glasses of water for us. I took a sip of mine and then asked Reilly, "What does Arno have against you? Why is this so personal?"

Reilly didn't answer, but I needed to know. "Please tell us. Maybe it will help."

After a long pause he finally spoke. "There's a lot of history between us, none of it good."

Clearly, Reilly wasn't up to the task of filling us in on his past, so I moved past the subject. "I just spoke with Greg Morgan and he's looking into the charges," I said, trying to cheer him up. "Don't give up, Sean. We can still clear your name."

"It doesn't matter anymore," Reilly said. "There's no coming back from this. And now you and Marco are being threatened with obstruction if you continue to investigate."

Just then the front door opened, allowing a bright stream of light to intersect the gloomy bar. A woman draped in shadow stood in the doorway. She pulled the sunglasses from her eyes and made her way toward us, letting the door glide shut behind her. And then I recognized her. It was Sean's fiancé, Marie Baker.

She was short, but still taller than me, with long, golden brown hair pulled around her ears. She was wearing a pale pink spring dress with short white heels. The only jewelry she wore was a modest but beautiful engagement ring.

Marie came up from behind Sean and touched his shoulder. He spun slowly and allowed her to wrap her arms around him, holding him tenderly. I met Marco on the opposite end of the bar. "What do we do now?"

"We wait for Reilly to leave and then plan our next move."

"Does it matter? Dylan has already been arrested. With Arno leading the charge it won't take long before he bullies a confession from him."

"That's the problem," Marco said. "Before you arrived, Reilly told me about an email he received from the tech specialist. He tracked Paige's phone to the site of a long-distance trucking company just outside of New Chapel city limits."

"How is that a problem?"

"Because Dylan Cutler didn't work there. Luke Hurst did."

I sat down on a stool at the bar, my thoughts swirling. "What does that mean?"

"It means we still have a potential suspect to interview."

"What about Dutch?" I asked. "How are we going to continue investigating if we're being threatened with obstruction?"

"It's a threat. That's all. He'll have a hard time stop us from working on a private case if we've been hired to do so. We have a license. But we're going to have to go about our work quietly so we don't cause any more trouble."

"I think we should talk to Dylan, too, find out what he knows."

"Do you really think they're going to let you into the jail after what happened?"

I thought for a moment, my mind flashing back to this past Christmas Eve when Marco and I, ignoring strict demands from Sergeant Reilly, had convinced Matron Patty to let us in to the jail to speak with one of the suspects in a kidnapping case. After being caught and thoroughly reprimanded, the station had completely revised its visitor policy.

"I'll call my dad and see if he can convince Patty to let us in," I said.

Marie walked over to us, leaving Reilly by himself at the other end of the bar. Her makeup was soft, her cheeks rubbed lightly with blush, mascara running slightly. She was a beautiful, mild-mannered woman, and I was at once happy and sad for Reilly. He had found the perfect woman to settle down and start a family with, but now, because of an old feud with a disgusting, dirty detective, Sean's future wasn't certain.

"Thank you so much for calling me," Marie said to Marco. "It's good to see you, Abby."

"Hi, Marie," I said and we shared a strong hug. "I'm sorry for what's happening, and I promise we won't stop until we fix this."

Marie looked heartened, but then looked back at her fiancé. "Has he been drinking?" she asked.

"No," Marco answered. "I just don't think he knows where else to go."

"I'll take him home," she said. "He doesn't have many close friends, but he holds both of you in the highest regard. We both really appreciate your help."

"Please call us if you need anything," I said.

"Or if you hear any new information," Marco added.

Marie nodded and then walked back to Sean, took his hand, and the two of them walked out of the bar together.

"Tonight we head to The Lost Weekend," Marco started. "I talked to the owner about an hour ago and he's seen Luke hanging out there every night. It's our best chance to find out something quickly."

"I'll go get some work done at Bloomers and ask Theda if she will take Seedy out for a walk tonight. I have a feeling we might be out late."

Marco lifted his hand for a high five, "Team Salvare, still on the case."

I slapped his hand. "How about a Turkey sandwich to go?"

At that moment my phone dinged and I immediately knew who it was.

Me: *Pinky swear is still in effect, just postponed temporarily. I promise.*

Jillian: *You can't blow me off forever. I know where you live.*

CHAPTER NINE

Just after eight o'clock that evening, we pulled into the gravel parking lot in front of a low wooden building with faded brown paint and an old-fashioned brown mansard roof. The nineteen seventies' style building looked tired and rundown, and when we stepped inside, we had to blink to see through the haze of smoke in the dimly lit room.

"I don't even want to breathe in here," I said. "I thought they banned smoking from bars."

"Not this bar," Marco said and nodded at the bartender. "This way."

A classic rock ballad was playing softly over the speakers. We bellied up to the bar and Marco shook hands with the owner. Behind him was a mirrored wall full of shelves and liquor bottles, some dusty and faded, some turned upside down with spigots on the ends, and a line of beer taps across the entire bottom row. "Abby, this is Gus Williams. Gus, this is my wife, Abby Knight Salvare."

"Any wife of Marco's is a friend of mine," he said with a firm, gritty handshake and a gristly voice. His full grey mustache fanned out as he gave me a wide smile. He bent down to grab a bottle and two glasses from behind the bar. "Marco helped me out of a real tricky situation a while back," he said and poured the golden liquor into the glasses. "This is the good stuff. On the house."

Marco handed me a glass and we clinked. He gave me his secret, sexy smile - knowing full well that I did not want to drink whatever it was I held in my hand - and downed his liquor. I put the glass to my lips and inhaled the sharp alcohol fumes. Not wanting to seem disrespectful, I held my breath and took a sip, trying unconvincingly to ignore the burn sliding down my throat.

"What can I do you two for?" Gus asked as he lit up a cigarette and let it hang between his lips.

Marco had already done his homework on Luke Hurst and had found him listed on several dating sights, along with a profile picture of a young, handsome man with a full head of light brown hair, a sharp nose, a trim beard, and a muscular build. He handed the picture to Gus and they began talking.

I slid around on the bar stool to survey our surroundings. There were a handful of men and women sitting down a few seats from us at the bar, some with their heads down, others watching the television hung above the mirrored wall. Across the room was a crowd of men playing pool at some of the tables, occasionally letting out a guttural laugh or a loud crack of the cue ball. There was even a small linoleum dance floor with a jukebox which one woman was leaned over, her black bra strap showing beneath the slim material of her tank top. She shook her hips to the beat and tapped her finger on the buttons, flipping through the music selection.

"That's him," Gus said, nodding his head toward one of the tables where three men were playing pool.

"He sure doesn't look much like his photo anymore," I said. He still had thick brown hair, but it had severely receded and was combed straight back off his forehead, making his face look larger and, with no beard, his jowly cheeks stand out. The slender nose I'd seen in the photo had gotten fleshier too, as had his stomach.

"Let's go have a seat by the pool tables," Marco said, handing me a beer. "Let's see what happens. Be sure to snap a photo of him."

I sat on a stool along the blacked-out windows as Marco walked up to one of the tables and said, "Care if I join the next game?"

"Grab a cue," one of the men said. "I'm just about to sink the winning shot." He leaned over, took aim, and knocked the eight ball into a corner pocket.

He fist-pumped in victory then slapped his hand on the table. "Six for six, boys. I'm unstoppable tonight. He chugged his beer and turned to Marco, exchanging a firm handshake. "You sure you're ready to take me on, new guy? The name's Bud."

"Marco Salvare," my hunky hubby said, looking hot and fit in a light blue T-shirt, tight navy jeans, and brown boots. He turned in my direction. "My wife, Abby."

"Nice to meet you, little lady," Bud said with a wink.

"Kent," another man said. He shook Marco's hand and gave me a nod. Several of the other men crowded around the pool table, and I began to feel uneasy. I was completely out of my element, but Marco could fit in just about anywhere. He was introduced around and made some of the guys laugh, which eased my mind. I felt safe with Marco. I always did.

Finally, Luke approached us. He shook Marco's hand and studied him curiously. "Luke Hurst," he finally said. "Don't I know you from somewhere?"

"Possibly," Marco said. "I own Down The Hatch."

I held my breath, wondering if Luke was going to put it together that Marco was also a private eye, but Gus saved the day.

"How about a round on the house?" Gus called, approaching with a grin. He set a tray full of opened beer bottles on the table. "Marco, my friend. Checking out the competition?"

"Actually, I'm thinking about adding a pool table," Marco said. He picked up a block of blue chalk and rubbed the end of his pool stick. "Bud and I were just about to play."

"Down The Hatch, yeah," Luke said and then looked around at the other men. "I've been kicked out of there a few times." That got everyone laughing except Marco, myself and Gus.

"Don't even think about starting anything here, Luke," Gus said and motioned to the baseball bat hanging behind the bar. "We don't kick people out around here."

"Eight ball," Luke said, grabbing the pool cue from Bud. "What do you say, Mark?"

"It's Marco," he corrected and began wracking the balls.

Bud took a seat, as did the other men who were now watching with interest. I took out my phone and snapped several photos surreptitiously, making sure I had a clear shot of our suspect.

Luke took the first shot and sank a few balls immediately. Marco shook his head, "What do you do for a living, Luke? Pool shark?"

"I'm a driver for a trucking firm."

"Which firm? Miller's?"

Luke took his shot and sank another ball. "What's it to you?"

"I have a buddy over at Miller's," Marco said. "Maybe you know him."

"I guess I should've said I *did* drive for a trucking firm," Luke said and missed his shot. "I got laid off a few weeks ago. Boss said I was one of the best, but he had too many drivers, and you know how that goes. The low man on the totem pole is always the first to go. Now, how about you stop stalling and take your shot."

Marco took aim and missed. "I thought about being a driver before I bought the bar, but decided it'd be too hard on my wife, being gone so much. How does your wife stand it?"

"I'm divorced." Luke snickered, lining up his shot. Then he said loud enough for everyone to hear, "Best thing that ever happened to me was to get rid of her."

I couldn't help but wonder how he meant that comment. "So it wasn't an amicable divorce?" I piped up, unable to stay quiet any longer.

Luke stopped and turned to me, propping his pool cue on the ground, "*Amicable?* Marco, you marry a dictionary or what?"

"She means was the divorce nasty or not," Marco explained.

"Oh, yeah. It got nasty all right," Luke explained. "She sold the house without telling me. Left me homeless. That's pretty nasty if you ask me."

"Did you keep in touch?" I asked.

Luke was just about to line up his cue again, but turned and gave me a haughty look, "We did keep in touch, yeah. Now let me ask you a question. Are you gonna let me finish my shot or you wanna keep yappin'?"

I gripped the bottom of my seat hoping it would keep me from popping like a top. Marco stepped over to grab his drink and gave me a pat on the knee. We watched as Luke took his time lining up his shot. He was clearly flustered and I had to keep reminding myself that we had to blend in, not stand out. Luke fired his shot which spun in the opposite direction he was aiming, causing him to swear and slam his fist on the table.

He had quite a temper.

Marco took aim and landed a striped ball in a side pocket. "You said you *did* keep in touch with her. Let me guess. Her husband found out."

Luke's demeanor shifted as did his grip on his pool cue. "I don't recollect telling you she had a husband."

So much for blending in.

"Why are you two so interested in my ex-wife?" Luke inched closer to Marco. "And I hope you got a real good reason."

The bar got quiet and several of the men behind Luke stood up from their seats.

Marco walked in front of me, his hands still on his pool cue. "We're just having a friendly game. We're just talking."

"I don't like the *way* you're talking," Luke said. A few more men came around the other side of the pool table and my heart started to race. "Why don't you tell me why you're really here, before things turn…*amicable*."

Marco hung up his stick and motioned for me to head toward the door.

"Where do you think you're going?" Luke asked.

"I need you to calm down and back up," Marco responded firmly. "We didn't mean any trouble. We'll just be on our way."

"Not so fast, pretty boy," Luke called after us. He and some of his buddies followed us out of the bar and across the parking lot. Before we could get in the car Luke grabbed Marco's arm and pushed him up against the window. "You're not going anywhere until you answer some questions."

"Abby," Marco said calmly. "Get in the car, please."

"I'm calling the police," I said loudly, my voice shaking.

Marco turned his head casually in my direction and smiled. I was immediately struck by the sight of Luke, boiling hot, holding Marco against the car and Marco's calm face smiling at me. I smiled back and nodded, got into the car, and watched from the passenger seat.

"That's a good boy. Don't want your wife to see you get beat up." He leaned in closer, pressing his arm against Marco's throat.

With one quick motion Luke Hurst was twisted around and dropped to the ground, Marco quickly wrestling Luke's second arm behind his back. The other men approached Marco, but he pulled Luke's wrist, wrenching a high-pitched yelp from the subdued thug.

"Tell them to back off."

"Back off right now," Luke said, "Back off."

I dialed 9-1-1 and leaned over to the driver's side window, my finger ready to press send.

"I'm going to ask you a few questions," Marco sneered, getting into his face. "And you're going to answer. Got me?"

Luke's adam's apple bobbed up and down as he swallowed. Putting on a brave face for his buddies, he asked, "What gives you the right?"

Marco pulled out his wallet and flashed his PI badge. "Now you can talk to me right now or I will make sure you never play pool with this hand again."

"What do you want from me?" he cried.

"Where were you at the time of Paige Rafferty's death?" Marco asked, still kneeling on his back, holding Luke's constricted arm.

"At the truck stop," Luke shot back.

"Where?"

"Off the interstate. The Over Night truck stop. Right up the road."

"How long have you been staying there?"

"About a month," he said.

"How did you hear about Paige's death?"

Luke paused for a long moment. Marco jerked his wrist again. "On the news," he winced.

"When was the last time you asked Paige for money?" Marco asked.

"Who said I asked her for money?"

"Her husband."

"Look, man, I never touched Paige. I wasn't there the day she was killed. I did ask her for money but that was weeks ago. I haven't been around to see her since she filed a restraining order against me."

"There," Marco said and stood up. "That wasn't so hard."

Luke got to his knees and spit on the ground. I saw him motion to his friends as Marco turned to me and nodded.

"Marco, watch out," I called, but it was too late. Two men rushed him and pushed him against the driver's side window, forcing me to jump back and lose grip on my cell phone. Just then I saw bright red and blue lights begin to flash, lighting up the whole parking lot.

Before the men could scatter, I saw officers coming out of nowhere and heard a scuffle in the gravel. How could they have gotten there so fast? My first thought was that Gus had called the police, but then I had my answer. Out of the red and blue shadows came a dark brown trench coat.

Dutch.

I retrieved my phone and met Marco outside of the car. The officers were busy handcuffing and taking away Luke Hurst and his two friends. Arno strolled up with hands deep inside his coat pockets with a big, cocky grin on his face. Marco was brushing the dust from his shirt and I looped my arm through his. "What are you doing here, Dutch?" I asked.

He smiled. "You're welcome, first of all. I just saved your husband from spending the night in jail. And second—"

"What are you talking about?" I asked defiantly. "Marco was defending himself."

Marco kept quiet and tapped my waist, discreetly begging me to keep my mouth shut.

"I saw the way you took down Luke," Arno said to my husband. "Three drunk men against one ex-Army Ranger. Doesn't seem like a fair fight to me."

"I appreciate the help, Detective," Marco said. "Are we free to go?"

"That's Detective *Sergeant* now."

"Not for long," I said.

"What's that?" Arno asked. "You're not being disorderly, now, are you?"

"You don't intimidate me, Dutch, and you can't stop us from investigating."

"Oh, you don't think so, huh?" Arno hitched up his belt and put his hands around his waist, pinning his coat back, revealing a service revolver holstered under his arm. "Not only can I charge you with interference, but I can slap on obstruction, refusing to obey a lawful order, and maybe even drunk and disorderly. You haven't been drinking tonight, have you Mrs. Salvare?"

"Are we free to go, Detective Sergeant?" Marco asked again.

"Sure, sure, you're free to go," Arno replied casually. "Just remember what I said, and try to be a little more careful. You're lucky we were here this time."

With my teeth grinding inside my clenched jaw, Marco walked with me around to the passenger side and opened my door.

"One more thing," Arno said and turned back toward us. "Tell Reilly I say hello."

"What do we do now?" I asked as Marco got behind the wheel. The red and blue lights were still silently flashing around the parking lot. "He knows Reilly hired us."

94

"But he can't stop us from investigating without an injunction," Marco said. "And that will have to go through the DA's office, which means we need to close this case quickly."

As we got back onto the road I asked, "Are you okay? They could've hurt you really badly, Marco."

"I've been through worse," he said and placed his free hand on mine. "*We've* been through worse. It's part of the job. That's why fitness training is so important."

"You know what we're going to do first thing tomorrow?" I asked, quickly changing the subject. "Pay a visit to that truck stop. They have to have security cameras. They can tell us whether or not Luke was really there on Monday."

"Good idea."

"Hey! We could even stop for breakfast first."

Marco gave me a side glance. "How about this instead? We'll head there right after our morning workout and a healthy breakfast of fruit and granola."

I sank back against the seat with a sigh. Goodbye, buttery blueberry pecan muffin. Hello intensive training session.

CHAPTER TEN

Friday

"Come on, Abby, one more set of push-ups. You can do it."

I pushed myself up and let myself flop back down, tasting the sweat pouring from my forehead.

"You don't have to grumble at me," Marco chided. "I'm just trying to help."

I scowled at my husband. "That wasn't me. It was my stomach. It needs food."

"It's going to get food right after you do one more set."

"One more set?" I exhaled and flopped back down again. "You are a cruel man. We've been at this for hours."

"You've exercised for twenty minutes, Buttercup."

"My muscles are on fire, Marco. I need to stop."

"Feel the burn," he said. "Let the burn push you forward. Pain is all in the mind."

I pushed my chest off the ground and felt the burn sear through my shoulders. I was exhausted but I worked through the pain and actually finished the set.

"Nice form."

I rolled onto my back with a groan.

Marco held out his hand and helped me to my feet. "You'll be bikini-ready in no time."

"I've never been bikini ready," I sighed. "Let's just focus on one-piece-ready."

"Well then," Marco smiled. "Let's do two sets of stairs and then we can eat."

"Cruel!" I called, as he started up the basement stairs ahead of me.

I'd barely made it to the top when Marco ran down past me without even breaking a sweat, giving me a pat on the rear as he passed by. "It's better than Jillian calling you Flabby Abby, isn't it?"

Once we'd had breakfast, showered, and got dressed, we headed out to check on Luke's alibi. I called Bloomers and let Lottie know I would be a little late, and then spent the rest of the car ride stretching my sore muscles and rolling my neck. We drove past The Lost Weekend and just a few miles beyond that was the Over Night truck stop, a large two-story gas station off of the highway with a parking lot the size of a football field.

I had never actually been to that gas station because it was always crowded with semis and oversized shipping trucks. We drove through the lot where the drivers would park their trucks and pulled into a parking spot just beside the gas station's front entrance. Marco pointed out several security cameras on the outside.

"If Luke was telling the truth then they must have some record of him here," I said. "The cameras are everywhere." Just then my phone rang. I pulled it from my pocket and said to Marco, "It's Greg Morgan. I need to take this."

"I'll go in and check the place out," Marco said. "Be right back."

Marco exited the car, and I watched his lean figure as he strolled in the front doors. "Hey, Greg. What did you find out?"

"That I shouldn't get involved in other people's cases," he said with his normal irreverent charm. "I was told in no uncertain terms by my boss to stay out of it."

"You're kidding. What did he say, exactly?"

"He said that Arno was on top of it, and the Chief of Police had faith in him closing the case soon."

"Did you even try to push the subject?"

"Believe me, I tried. Sorry, Abby."

"What about Sergeant Reilly?" I asked. "I will testify in court that Connor MacKay falsified his sources in order to write that article."

"Abby, Reilly is being investigated by Internal Affairs." Greg stopped talking to let the weight of that settle. "I don't know what he did, but this is serious. MacKay's article is the least of his concerns now."

"He didn't do anything wrong," I argued. "I was there."

"I believe you."

"Do you also believe me now that Arno has it out for Reilly?" I asked.

"I do."

"And?"

"There's nothing I can do."

I tried my hardest to keep my composure as I thanked Morgan for taking the time to help me. Even though it seemed like sometimes I was talking to a brick wall, I knew he was being honest, but before he hung up, I stopped him. "Greg, wait. What if I could prove that Detective Arno was mishandling this case? Could you do anything then?"

He thought for a long moment. "If you can prove that Arno is purposefully construing evidence for his own personal gain, maybe. But how are you going to do that?"

"Don't worry about how," I said. "You just get the paperwork ready to file."

"What paperwork?"

"Just do it, Morgan."

"Whatever you say, Knight. Good luck."

I put my phone away and felt the muscles in my shoulders tense up all over again.

Marco didn't have the same confident stride as he walked back toward me. He opened the door and plopped down into his seat. "They won't cooperate. First, the attendant told me the surveillance video is scrubbed daily. Then, when I asked to speak to the manager, he told me that someone had already picked up the video records."

"Do you think Dutch came by?"

"Probably," he replied, "but as soon as I flashed my P.I. badge the manager closed up, wouldn't tell me anything."

"What do we do now?"

"There's a second story where the truck drivers can wash up and relax. If we could get up there and ask around, I'm sure someone would have information about Luke."

"Maybe I could get up there."

99

"How?"

"The attendant and the manager, are they both men?"

"Yeah, does that matter?"

"You bet it does." I pulled the passenger's side visor down and checked my makeup. I pulled a few fingers through my hair and turned to Marco. "Leave this to me."

Upon entering the gas station's front doors, I first spotted the restroom sign just beyond the checkout counter. The store was fairly busy with customers and I noticed that there were cameras in each of the four corners of the convenience area. An unfriendly face greeted me as I walked slowly by the counter, pretending to peruse the candy and gum selection. Then, with a quick glance over my shoulder, I casually entered the short hallway leading to the restrooms and entered through the women's door. Just as I had hoped, the bathroom had only one toilet and the door was lockable from the inside.

I worked quickly, stuffing single-ply toilet paper into the dirty, yellowed toilet bowl. As soon as the roll was empty, I flushed a few times for good measure. The bowl filled with water and I dashed out of the room heading straight for the counter. "I'm sorry but the women's toilet is out of order. Do you have another restroom I could use?"

The attendant was busy ringing up several people standing in line. "Use the men's."

I hadn't expected that. The attendant continued his work behind the register and I waited impatiently for a break in the line. "Excuse me, but I don't feel comfortable using the men's bathroom. Can I —"

Before I could continue, the man who I assumed to be the manager approached me. "Is there a problem?"

"The women's toilet is out of order and I'm kind of in a rush," I lied. "Is there another bathroom I could use?"

"Sure," he said. "You can use the men's. I'll make sure it's empty."

"No," I stopped him. "I don't feel comfortable using the men's bathroom."

A loud buzzing noise came from the back room behind the coolers, and the manager seemed to become agitated. "Give me a minute and I'll clean the bathroom for you."

"It's sort of an emergency," I said, feigning embarrassment.

The buzzer sounded again. "I understand. I'll be right with you."

"It's a *female* emergency," I emphasized.

With that the manager straightened his collar as if he had been wearing a tie, visibly uncomfortable. He pointed to the back stairwell. "Up the stairs and down the hallway to your left. Please make it quick."

The floorboards creaked as I made my way up the darkened stairwell. There were uncovered bulbs hanging on the wall above me that barely lit a path down the hallway. To my right were rows of washers and dryers, all churning methodically, and above them were coin-operated vending machines with small packets of detergent, fabric softener and other random toiletries.

Beyond that was an opened door to my right. I peeked inside to see several men and women lounging in the dark watching television. The volume was low and there were a few curious looks my way, but I decided to continue looking around before interrupting. Down the dimly lit hallway to my left was the bathroom. Around the corner was another hallway with rows of white doors. I stopped to inspect one and realized that they were individual shower rooms.

One of the doors opened and out stepped a man with wet, messy hair, wearing only a towel. I didn't have to fake embarrassment as our eyes locked. The man gave me an odd look and stepped into a room across from the showers. I turned around and made my way back toward the bathroom.

"Hey there, stranger," a woman said. She was leaning up against the bathroom door with her arms crossed, giving me a peculiar smile. "I noticed you sneaking around the place, thought you might like a tour."

"Actually," I said, trying to feel her out. "I'm kind of looking for someone."

"You, too?" she asked casually. "Follow me."

She led me back toward the TV room. Her blond hair was up in a pony-tail and she was wearing a sleeveless American flag t-shirt. I wasn't sure if she had heard me correctly, or if she knew who I was looking for, but she sat down next to a thin, bald man, sprawled out on one of the sofas in front of the television and said, "Little lady here is looking for someone."

The man straightened up a bit. "You lookin' for Luke, too?"

"Yes," I said. "Do you know him?" I pulled out my phone and showed him the picture I had secretly taken of Luke at the pool hall.

"We all know Luke," he said, motioning around the room at the other drivers. "But, like I told the other guy, you won't find him around here no more."

"What other guy?" I asked. "Was it a detective?"

102

"Sure," he replied. "Came up here in his big overcoat, askin' after Luke. Told me not to talk to you, too. I can tell you that. He described you and everything, red hair and all. He doesn't much care for you."

"No," I agreed, "he doesn't, but it's important I talk to you."

"Go right ahead. My name's Randy, by the way."

"Abby Salvare," I said as I flipped through my phone, looking for the photos of Luke I had taken at the bar. "Was the detective here this morning?"

"No, no. He came through yesterday."

I showed the photo of Luke to Randy. "Can you tell me if this is the same Luke?"

"Sure is."

"Was he here Monday night, around six?"

He licked his lips and lifted his finger, as if it would help him recall, "He was here in the afternoon talking about making some quick money. Haven't seen him since."

"Do you live here?" I asked, then immediately regretted the question.

He laughed along with a few other people. "Yeah, I guess you could say that. Not supposed to, but Luke and I have been stayin' here since we got laid off from Miller's. Now, speakin' of Miller's, here's something else I told that detective. Luke's been talkin' about knocking over that place since we got canned, but I didn't think he had it in him. Then he comes around here, wanting me to get involved. Now, listen. I'm a driver, not a robber, so I told him to scoot."

"And that was Monday?"

"Yes, ma'am."

I thanked Randy, handed out a few of our cards, and slipped back down the stairwell and out the front doors. Marco was outside of the car next to the driver's door with an exasperated look on his face. "What took you so long?"

I got into the passenger side while Marco sat down next to me and closed his door.

"I've been trying to call you and then realized you forgot your phone. You have a text from Jillian, too, by the way."

"I'm sorry. I didn't realize I was gone that long, but I did get some great info."

We discussed my conversation on the ride back, highlighting the fact that Luke was not at the gas station as he had claimed, and that Dutch now had the video files, the only proof of Luke's whereabouts before the murder. "Maybe he made one final attempt to extract money from Paige before resorting to robbing Miller's?"

Marco's eyes were forward, watching the road as he shook his head. "But where does Dylan come into play? He was caught with Paige's computer and wedding ring."

"There has to be more to the story," I said, "some piece that ties it all together. Luke and Dylan don't know each other, as far as we know, but they both seem to be involved."

"Okay," Marco started. "We have two suspects; Dylan and Luke. Dylan was caught with Paige's belongings, but her cell phone was traced to Luke's former place of employment, the same place he was talking about robbing. Both men are being held in jail right now, and both are probably being questioned in Paige's murder, so where does that leave us?"

I couldn't answer right away. The intrepid investigator in me wanted to keep searching for clues and finish solving the mystery. There were too many questions to just stop now. But both of our top suspects were already in jail. Knowing Dutch, he would have a confession in no time. Whether or not the real murderer was put behind bars didn't matter to him, as long as he closed the case fast. But Marco was right. Where did that leave us? "Are you suggesting we stop investigating?"

"What more can we do?"

"I don't know, but we can't leave it up to Dutch."

"Sunshine, listen. We started this case to help Reilly, and look what's happened. We've only made things worse. Arno has the upper hand here. He has the chief of police and the district attorney on his side. He has our top suspects in custody. I don't like the man, but I think he's got us beat this time."

My phone rang, giving me a good reason not answer Marco right away. I wasn't about to stop investigating, and as I answered the phone I crossed my fingers, hoping my dad was calling with good news."

CHAPTER ELEVEN

"Bad news," my dad started, to my utter disappointment. I put him on speaker phone so Marco could hear. "Patty can't get you and Marco in to speak to Dylan."

My heart sank. I looked at my husband with a frown and he patted my knee. Maybe Marco was right. Maybe the best thing we could do now was to back off the case and not get into any more trouble. I could focus my attention instead on Reilly and the police department, talk to the captain, and force some legal recourse if I had to.

"But I do have good news," he continued. "She can get you in alone, but you have to follow the new procedures. You have to go during visiting hours and your conversation will be monitored."

"That's fantastic news!" I cried out in joy. "I'll go right now."

"What about dinner tonight?" my dad reminded me. "Your mother is making something special for us."

"Yes, of course," I said. "We'll be over just before six. I'm hungry already. Thanks again, Dad. I'll see you tonight."

Marco drove past Bloomers and Down The Hatch, heading directly for the jail. "Maybe Arno doesn't have us beat just yet," he said. "I should never doubt you, Sunshine. I'll be at work if you need me."

. . .

Upon entering the jail, I was met by Matron Patty, who guided me through the security check, did a quick search of my purse, had me leave my cell phone in a locker, and took me straight to the visitors' room. I sat in a plastic chair in a row of walled-off compartments and waited. Within minutes, Dylan was brought into the room on the opposite side of the glass wearing his orange prison garb, shackled ankles, and black rubber flip-flops.

His head was shaved down to the scalp, eyes framed with large dark circles. He had the long, narrow face of his mother, but thinner and pale. On his arms were dark blue bruises. He sat down and picked up the phone with one hand, his other tapping anxiously on the plastic countertop.

My first task was to gain his confidence. "Hi, Dylan. My name is Abby. I'm here to help you."

He twisted in his chair and held the phone loosely to his ear, his hand shaking. "Then get me out of here."

"I'm not a lawyer," I said. "I'm a private investigator. I'm going to ask you a few question and I need you to answer honestly."

In fact, both of his hands were shaking, and his words came out slowly. "I just need to get out of here. I'm not gonna make it. Are you police?"

"No." I tried to explain myself. "I'm not with the police department. I used to work for a public defender and I know how the system works. Have you been assigned a public defender yet?"

"I don't know. I don't think so." He sniffled and wiped his nose on his sleeve. "Can you get my mom?"

"Dylan, listen to me. You're going to have to demand a lawyer. It's your right to have representation. Whatever you do, just sit tight and keep your mouth shut. Do you understand?"

"What about my mom?"

"Dylan, focus."

"Can you please get my mom?"

"No, I can't" I said, "but I can get a message to her."

"Tell her that I need help," he said quietly.

"I'm trying to help you right now."

He studied me for a moment. His eyes were unfocused as he sized me up, stopping briefly at my chest which I immediately covered. He closed his eyes.

"Dylan."

"Why do you want to help me?" he asked, slowly blinking at me.

"Because I don't like to see young people railroaded by detectives who should know better. Did anyone read you your rights when you were arrested?"

He scratched his scalp. "I don't remember. I was asleep. Next thing, they had me on the floor handcuffing me."

"What time was that?"

"I don't know. Morning."

"How did they enter your house?"

"I don't know."

"Did they read you your rights?"

"They were yelling at me. That's all I remember."

"Did they bring you directly to the police station?"

"Yeah, they stuck me in a room and questioned me all day."

"Do you know who they were?"

He nodded as his expression noticeably soured, snapping him out of his daze. His fist closed, and he struck his thigh like he was punishing himself.

"Was it Detective Arno?" I asked.

He continued to punch his thigh and his eyes welled up.

"Dylan, stop. What was he questioning you about?"

"He wasn't questioning me. He was telling me to confess, threatening me, but I didn't kill her."

"Were you friends with Paige Rafferty?"

He nodded, his eyes now streaming with tears. "And he kept telling me to admit that I strangled her and robbed her. I swear to God I didn't do it."

"Were you at Mrs. Rafferty's house on Monday?"

He began looking around the room as if someone was watching him. "I can't go back to prison. I won't make it one day in there."

"Dylan, answer my question. Focus, please. Did you visit Mrs. Rafferty on Monday?"

"I don't remember if it was Monday. Mrs. Rafferty didn't have any work for me, but she had some fruit for my mom."

"Were you at her front or back door?"

"Front door."

"What did she give you?"

"A bag of fruit. I don't know. I can't tell you any more." He leaned his head against the glass that divided us and repeated, "I can't."

"Why did you have Paige's stolen items?"

"I can't say anymore. You have to get my mom."

"What about Paige's cell phone. Do you remember seeing it?"

"Stop asking me questions," Dylan cried. "I've said too much already."

"This is the only way I can help. You need to focus and try to remember something or there's nothing I can do. Think really hard, Dylan. Did the detective have you sign anything?"

He wiped his eyes with his sleeve. "He wanted me to sign something, but I didn't. My mom told me never to sign anything."

Matron Patty cleared her throat from behind me. "Abby, time to go."

I gave her a nod and turned back to Dylan. "I have to leave now, but I'll make sure to get that message to your mom."

"Tell her I know who did it," he said. His eyes were clear now and desperately locked onto mine as he continued quietly. "Tell her to check the cameras."

"Say that again?" I asked in shock.

"Abby?" Matron Patty called.

I held up my index finger behind me, asking for another minute. "Tell me who did it." I demanded.

The police guard came into view and stood behind Dylan. He instructed him to hang up the phone.

"Wait a minute," I called through the glass. "Tell me who murdered Paige."

Dylan looked over my shoulder and his eyes widened.

"Wait, Dylan. What cameras?"

Dylan looked away quickly. He hung up the phone, stood up, and was shuffled out of the room. My thoughts spinning, I turned to ask Patty for more time, but my eyes were instead met by the blazing hot gaze of Detective Richard *Dutch* Arno.

"You're in a whole mess of trouble now," he said.

"She followed all of the rules, Detective Sergeant," Patty intervened, trying to ease the situation. "She's well within her rights."

"Interrogating my suspect in the middle of an ongoing investigation?"

"I wasn't interrogating anyone," I insisted. "He hasn't been charged, has he?"

"Stop interfering with my case or I swear to God —"

"Start doing your job properly and I won't have to."

"I will have you and your husband thrown in jail. And your good buddy, Sean Reilly? I'll make it so that he won't even be able to work security in this town. No more warnings. You leave this case alone or I make your life a living hell."

"No deal."

He breathed in deeply, like a bellows about to stoke a fire, and grumbled, "Then the next time you see me will be in court. You can expect a subpoena from the DA's office."

I stood firm as I fired back my response. "You just better hope that you find the real killer before I do, or the next time I see you will be behind bars."

"Get her out of here!" he commanded.

Patty escorted me swiftly from the room to collect my belongings. I was fuming inside. Then I noticed Patty holding her hand over her mouth and thought at first that she was in shock over what I'd said. Then I noticed she was hiding a smile.

"I've never seen anyone talk to him like that," she said. "Well done." But her expression turned serious as she continued. "I need to warn you, though, Abby, Arno's deadly serious. You should probably be prepared for a battle."

"I'll talk to Greg Morgan," I said.

"Maybe you should also talk to your father," she added. "He will have some insight. I think you should know exactly who you're going up against."

. . .

I relayed my altercation with Marco over the phone as I walked back to Bloomers. After he had calmed me down, we discussed Dylan's interrogation with Dutch, his current state, and odd behavior. We also concluded the mystery of the discarded bag of apples, but something still wasn't sitting right. "And before I left, Dylan said something really strange."

"What was that?" Marco asked.

"He wanted his mother to *check the cameras*. What do you think he means by that?"

"I'm not sure. Did you ask him?"

"He was taken away before I had time." I pulled my car into a spot around the corner from my shop and parked. I sat in the car and rolled my aching shoulders. "I believe him, Marco. I think he knows who killed Paige. He's scared for his life and I'm pretty sure it's because of Arno."

"Why don't you give Darlene a call and relay the message," Marco suggested, "see what she has to say."

I gave Marco a kiss over the phone and then pulled up a list of recently dialed numbers. After tapping the number for Darlene's office and turning on the speaker, I rolled up the windows and exited my car. The temperature outside was warming up and I was starting to roast in my faded denim and light yellow button-down shirt. I untucked the shirt and noticed that my pants were loose. I was so shocked that I almost didn't reply back when Darlene's secretary answered my call.

"I'm sorry, yes, Abby Knight Salvare calling for Darlene Cutler, please." I was put on hold as I made my way around the corner, stopping just before I got to Bloomers. The sign above the door still read, *Abby Knight, proprietor.* I really needed to get that sign changed to my married name, but at that moment it wasn't important. I stared at myself in the flower shop's large bay window.

"I'm sorry," came the receptionist's voice, "but Dr. Cutler is busy at the moment. May I take a message?"

"Do you know when she will be free?" I asked, still staring at myself, turning to catch a profile view. "I just need a minute."

"She's booked all day," the woman answered. "I can tell her that you called."

"Would you give her a message, please? It's from her son."

"Go ahead."

"He asked her to check the cameras. I'm trying to understand what he meant by that and I would really appreciate a call back as soon as possible."

"I will give her the message."

I entered Bloomers with a renewed confidence in myself. Not only had I stood up to one of the biggest bullies I had ever encountered, but also, all of those bland salads and rigorous exercise routines were actually paying off. I was losing weight, and quickly. I felt fantastic, and then I wondered, just for a brief moment, how much better I would feel if I actually *did* do Pilates with Jillian. I even considered calling her to resurrect our pinky swear, but before I could, my phone rang. It was Darlene Cutler.

"We need to talk," she said briskly, as if walking and talking. "I think Dylan is in way over his head and I may need your help."

"What can I do?"

"Meet me at my house tonight at nine," she said. "I'll explain everything then."

After I hung up with Darlene I realized that I was standing in the middle of Bloomers. Lottie was propped up against the checkout counter, Grace was standing in the doorway between the shop and the tea parlor, and Rosa's face was poking out through the workroom curtain. Bloomers was empty and there were only a few customers having tea in the parlor.

"Okay," I started. "Let me fill you in."

CHAPTER TWELVE

"Abracadabra," my dad said from his wheelchair, using his favorite childhood nickname for me. He was in the hallway behind my mom who had opened the door for us. After giving my mom a hug and my dad a kiss on the cheek, we were welcomed into the living room until dinner was ready. Suspiciously, though, there was no wafting aroma of freshly cooked food coming from the kitchen. My stomach rumbled in consternation.

It was comforting being back in my childhood home. I perused the familiar old family photos on the mantle above the fireplace, as always, horrified by my senior picture. I noticed an older family photo taken before my dad had his debilitating injury. He was standing tall and proud behind me, with one hand on my shoulder and another around my mom's waist, as if memorializing the fact that he was always there for us, and would always protect us.

My dad had been shot in the back by a fleeing fugitive, fracturing his spine, causing him to leave the force early and spend the rest of his life in a wheelchair. The man who'd shot my father was never caught, and every time I thought of the cold case, I knew that eventually, no matter where this man ended up, I would find him and bring him to justice. I breathed in to calm myself.

Dad had his recliner in front of the television, still littered with police magazines and reading glasses, and mom had one entire bookshelf dedicated to her myriad of art projects and published children's novels. Mom brought out some lemon water and my dad fidgeted nervously in his chair.

"Not this again, Maureen," he said.

"Hush, Jeffrey. It's good for you. Marco, don't you listen to him."

Marco lifted his glass, and his eyebrows, as we both noticed the ever so tiny red swirl in his ice cold lemon water.

I lifted my glass to the lamp light and asked. "What is it?"

"It's lemon water," she said emphatically, but watched carefully as I raised the glass to my lips. "with tabasco sauce."

"Ugh, no." I insisted. "No thank you."

"It gets the metabolism running and helps burn calories, even as you eat," mom claimed. "Try a sip before you say no."

I looked at Marco, and then at my dad as we all watched the red swirl dissipate inside our glasses. Marco took the first sip. I followed and let the liquid reside momentarily inside my closed jaw before swallowing. "Oh my God." My throat began to spasm involuntarily. "How much tabasco sauce did you use?"

Marco puckered his lips and set the glass down. "It's…an interesting combo."

"Well, it's my own recipe," she answered. "I don't know what all the fuss is about. I drink it every morning."

Mom returned to the kitchen and dad just smiled and shook his head. "She really does."

We chatted for a bit, catching up on our lives and then I steered the conversation toward the murder investigation. Before we really had a chance to dive in, mom called us into the kitchen. After settling around the table, my stomach now churning, Mom brought out a big glass bowl and set it down in front of us.

"Dinner is served," she said proudly.

"Salad is *not* dinner," my dad retorted to which she simply waved him away.

"We need to be in tip top shape for our cruise," she reminded. "This is a hearty salad, Jeffery. We will all be plenty satiated by the end of the meal."

I had to laugh as Marco turned to me first, then to my mom with an incorrigible smile. "It looks delicious, Maureen."

As we crunched away at our hearty salads, we filled my parents in on the entire investigation, not only ours, but Detective Arno's as well.

My dad ladled more dressing onto his second helping of salad before going back over the key elements of our case. "You have three suspects in my opinion, including Mr. Rafferty," he said. "I'm just wondering why he was so adamant about getting those cruise tickets back."

"For a refund, I'm assuming," I replied. "They would have been on the same boat as us."

My mom put a hand to her heart. "So sad," she whispered.

"You'd think there would be more pressing concerns than a refund on cruise tickets," he continued. "But I don't know the man."

"If Arno's cleared him then we can safely assume he had no other option," Marco added. "He was pushing hard for Slade's conviction. That's why Reilly's in this mess."

"It's a damn shame," Dad said. "I've worked with Reilly since he was a kid. Nineteen, I think, when he and Arno joined the force."

"Can you tell us why they don't get along?" I asked. "Reilly won't tell us and it's driving me crazy."

My dad sat back and placed his hands on the arms of his wheelchair, assuming his normal storytelling pose. "It was my first year as Sergeant when they joined the force. Arno was the hotshot, always needing to prove himself, and Reilly was the tall, gawky boy scout. They were good officers, balanced each other out, good cop, bad cop, all that.

"But you have to understand something about those two. They were best friends before they joined, then they became partners. I never saw the two men apart. We worked for years as a solid team. I watched them move up the ranks quickly, eventually being promoted to detective, and that's when things took a turn. I believe it was their first missing persons investigation."

My dad closed his eyes and shook his head. "A young girl, Beverly Polite, walking home from school, and just like that she was gone." He snapped his fingers and opened his eyes, looking at me. "We all knew who did it. His name was Jacob Barnes. He had a substantial criminal history, same MO, same everything. They found her school bag just one block from the Barnes' home, found her bloodied school uniform in a dumpster nearby, but never found the body.

"Barnes had a weak alibi, but all of the evidence was circumstantial. Not a single witness came forward. With no body and no witnesses, Arno couldn't get the DA to convene a grand jury and the case went cold. Poor guy, he was hung up on that case for years. I've seen the same thing happen to a lot of good detectives. Some guys spend the rest of their lives chasing that one cold case."

"Something bad must have happened between Arno and Reilly," I said.

"Yeah, well, two years later we get a new lead and it puts Jacob Barnes just within reach. It was him. This guy did it and everyone knew it, but there just wasn't enough evidence to convince the DA.

"Then Reilly came to me one night saying that Arno had left the evidence room with Beverly's school bag. We stopped Arno a few blocks from the Barnes' house. He was caught with one of her school books in the passenger seat. We knew what he was up to, planting evidence, but we didn't file charges against him. Looking back, I think maybe that was a mistake."

"What happened with the case?" I asked.

"Nothing," Dad answered. "Still cold. Barnes is a free man and Arno never forgave us for it. I know it must have crushed Reilly to rat on his partner, but hey, the man was doing his job. He's an honest cop."

"But Dutch is a dirty cop and now he's going after us," I began. "He's taking us to court with a whole list of charges."

"Abby, I know I've told you this before, but I need you to listen this time," my dad said firmly. "I want you to back off this case, and I want you to make it a point to tell Detective Arno that you're stepping away. If you and Marco get caught up in a court battle with him, it won't end well. I know a few people who might be able to help you out. I can make some calls, but once this battle starts, there's no stopping it. Do you hear me?"

"I do, Dad. I hear you." But my heart burned inside my chest setting off a chain reaction inside my body. My muscles tensed and my eyes started to tear up. "But I can't stop now. I was so close to preventing this murder. She would be alive if hadn't been late for that delivery."

My dad reached over and held my hand. "What happened is not your fault. You are the bravest young woman I have ever met, and I'm not just saying that because you're my daughter."

"Abigail," mom said. "Listen to your father."

"But bravery and justice have a limit," he concluded. "Don't let this case take you to a place you can't come back from. That's what happened to Arno, and I won't watch it happen to you. Reilly may be hurting right now, but he'll come out of this just fine. You've done all you can."

After dinner, Marco and I sat inside my cherished 1960 yellow Corvette convertible with my key hanging from the ignition. We had driven to my parent's house with the top down, enjoying the warm spring evening, but as we sat there in the driveway, the sun hanging low on the horizon, my spirits crushed, I couldn't bring myself to even start the engine.

Marco held my hand. "Your dad has a point."

"But justice shouldn't have a limit," I shot back. "We can't just walk away from something we know isn't right."

I knew what Marco was going to say. He was the cool-headed, responsible partner in this team. And I knew that my dad was right. What good would solving this case do if Marco and I both wound up in court, or worse, in jail? We could lose everything. Arno seemingly had the whole justice system on his side. How could we fight against that? I looked over at my husband and waited for his response.

Marco looked back at me with his kind, loving eyes and his warm smile and said, "You have a point, too, Sunshine. Let's go solve this case."

Was I hearing him right? My back straightened slightly and I felt his grip strengthen around my hand. "Really?" I asked.

"We haven't lost a case yet, and I'll be damned if Dutch is the one who takes us down."

My spirits lifted immediately and I twisted that key and revved the engine. "I love you."

Darlene hadn't arrived home from work by the time we parked in front of her house, so Marco and I took the opportunity to jaunt across the street to pay Mr. Rafferty a quick visit. The once beautiful, brightly lit mansion was now dark and gloomy. We walked up the path and noticed a maroon sedan parked in the driveway. Before we had a chance to ring the doorbell, a man exited the car and approached us on the darkened porch.

Marco let out a long, quiet sigh and whispered, "Let me handle this one."

The short, stubby man came into view and stepped up to greet us. "Ah, Marco Sal-Avare."

"It's *Salvare*," Marco responded.

"I know, it's just so hard to pronounce."

"Not that hard," Marco said.

"This must be Mrs. Sal-Varay." He stuck out his pudgy hand and his dimples protruded through doughy cheeks. "Vincent Wong," he said cordially as I shook his hand. His jet black hair was parted in the middle and his stubby black tie stopped well above the belt. He then held out a billfold in front of his face. "Private Eye."

"Let me guess," Marco started. "Mr. Rafferty hired you to find Paige's killer."

Vince stuck out his thumb at Marco and laughed in my direction. "Can't pull anything over on this guy. No wonder I'm always the second choice."

Before Marco could respond, Vince continued, "No, no. It's okay. I'm happy picking up the breadcrumbs. It pays the bills, and hey, no better way to follow a trail than with breadcrumbs. Am I right?"

His innocent cheeriness was met with solemn disdain as Marco hurried the conversation along. "Is Mr. Rafferty at home?"

Vince made a show of checking for clues around the front door. "What do you think, Sherlock?" His sarcasm was equally matched with innocuous charm.

"We just have a few questions," Marco said. "Why did Arno release him as a suspect?"

"Not to *toot* my own horn, but I did a little digging around the site where Rafferty was supposedly meeting this mysterious Mr. Smith and found multiple traffic cams

123

confirming his alibi." He finished with a tooting motion and smiled proudly.

"Do you know anything about that coffee cup Mr. Rafferty threw against the Cutler's front door?" I asked, still haunted by the very first clue I had noticed at the crime scene.

"Yes, and I may be responsible for that," he smiled and blushed as though he were the one who threw it. "That was a different mug. Mr. Rafferty and I were conducting a recreation of the scene inside his home, but instead of coffee, my client was imbibing a different type of liquid, if you know what I mean. Things got a little out of hand. I shouldn't have left him alone."

"Any idea what happened to the original mug?" I asked.

"I'm sure forensics has it. They did a thorough sweep of the house, left it quite a mess from what I saw."

"That's all we needed to know," Marco said. "Thanks."

As we walked away Vince continued, "You'll also be happy to know that the diamonds found in the street behind Rafferty's house were actually fake, most likely from the cell phone cover he had purchased for his wife. Still no phone, though."

"That's great, Vince," Marco said without turning around. "Good work."

"Thanks, Marco, and one of these days," he added. "I'm going to get that last name right."

As soon as we were out of Vince's earshot I said, "What was that about, grumpy?"

"He's a good guy, just a little—" Marco stopped himself.

"What?" I gave him a playful jab. "He's sweet."

"He's annoying."

I looped my arm through his as we walked across the street. "Aw, Marco's arch nemesis, the annoying Vincent Wong, private eye."

CHAPTER THIRTEEN

Darlene's garage began to open and we watched her SUV pull into the driveway. We met her by the car and she greeted us professionally, leading us inside through the garage. Her home was decorated with an intelligent, monotone coldness, almost as if we were entering a giant, sophisticated igloo. The color scheme was that of an iceberg, with bright whites, dirty grays, and brilliant shades of blue.

She sat with us in the living room and got straight to the point. "Dylan has been working as an informant for the police department. I couldn't say anything earlier, but now I think he's in way over his head. I'm worried that the detectives might out him as a snitch if he doesn't cooperate."

"Have you talked to him at the jail?" I asked.

"They wouldn't let me in to see him," she answered. "I was told to come back during visiting hours, which is impossible because of my practice. That's why I need your help. I need to know exactly what Dylan said to you."

I quickly replayed the interview in my head. "He said that he was at the Rafferty's house on Monday. Detective Arno was trying to get him to sign something, but he didn't. He said you told him never to sign anything. Then he said he knew who did it and asked you to check the cameras. Do you know anything about these cameras?"

"Yes," she responded sincerely. "He must think he caught someone."

"Tell us about the cameras," Marco said.

"Dylan installed them around the house," she began, once again tapping her heel rhythmically against the dark grey satin couch. "Ever since he was let out of prison there have been robberies all across our neighborhood. I didn't believe him when he told me he wasn't involved. Apparently Detective Arno didn't either, so Dylan bought the cameras and hid them around the house. If he's telling the truth, then they could prove his innocence."

"How is Arno involved?" I asked.

"He's the one who convinced my son to become a prison informant," she answered," in exchange for a shortened sentence. Ever since he was released Detective Arno has been harassing him about these robberies."

"So Dylan put up the cameras to provide an alibi?" Marco asked.

"No," she corrected. "He claims that the detective physically assaults him when he doesn't give him the information he wants." She bit her trembling lower lip and stiffened her chin, trying desperately to ward off an emotional outpouring. "He would come home with these dark bruises on his wrists and face. I didn't..." She caught herself before breaking into tears. "I didn't believe him."

Darlene Cutler presented herself as a cold, calm, professional woman, a mother who had given up on her son, but as I sat near her I could feel the heat from her body. Her cheek was warm as I consoled her and she wrapped her arms firmly around me, shaking deeply, her sobbing now uncontrollable.

I thought back to the dark bruises I saw on Dylan's wrists. I knew that Richard Arno was a bully and a corrupt detective, but holding Darlene, sensing the fear radiating from her, and hearing the stories of physical abuse against her son, I had a whole new level of disgust for the man. Now I knew that deep down inside, I would do anything to solve this case and make Dutch pay for his crimes.

She tried to continue through heavy breaths, "I'm afraid they're going to send him back to prison. I'm afraid he's going to die in there."

Marco excused himself as I held Darlene and let her cry. I could see him scanning the surroundings, walking around the living room picking up picture frames and searching the numerous rows of bookshelves along one of the walls. He left the room briefly, just long enough for Darlene to catch her breath and calm down.

"Can we take a look at the videos?" Marco asked, joining us again in the living room.

"I don't know how to operate them, but I can show you where they are."

Darlene guided us, pointing out the locations of all six security cameras Dylan had placed around their home. Finally, after retrieving the last memory card from the camera in Dylan's bedroom, we promised Darlene that we would do everything we could to help her son.

"I don't know how to thank you," she said, retrieving her purse from the counter as we were heading out. "I don't have much cash on me."

"Don't worry about that," Marco said. He handed her a card. "If anyone comes to your door — anyone at all — call the police first, then call us."

"I will," she said.

As I pulled away from the curb outside of Darlene's house, Marco started to shift in his seat slightly, his eyes darting from the rearview to the passenger side mirror. "Hand me your purse," he said.

"What's wrong?" I asked. I quickly pulled the small clutch from around my body and handed it over.

Marco took the memory cards and secured them in a zippered outside pocket. "I think we're being followed," he answered. "Don't look back."

I sat still with my eyes forward, instantly fighting the overwhelming urge to turn around. I didn't notice any headlights behind us, just the steady pace of street lamps above, casting glares across the convertible's windshield. "How do you know?"

"They're about two blocks back, headlights off. They pulled onto the road just after we did."

"What should I do?" I asked.

"Just keep driving. It looks like a sedan, probably Vince tailing us."

I pulled the wispy hairs from my face as the cool night breeze flowed through the open top. "Why would he be following us?"

"I told you," Marco replied. "He's annoying, probably wants to know what we're up to. Pull over when you can. We'll put the top up and see what he does."

I came to a stop and began the process of pulling up the top. Marco popped off his seatbelt and exited the car. I noticed the sedan a few blocks back with its headlights off. As soon as Marco got out, the car turned at an intersection. After the top was secured, Marco entered the car and we drove away. But two streets farther down he cursed under his breath.

"I see him now," I said. "What do I do?"

Marco thought for a second, still checking the mirrors and then said, "Maybe it's not Vince."

There was only one other person I could think of who would be on our tail. "Do you think it's Dutch?"

"It could be," he answered. "We should try to lose him."

"How?"

"Make a quick right turn. No signal."

"Where?"

"Here."

I followed Marco's directions, making quick turns, zig-zagging through neighborhoods and doubling back onto our main course. I was sure we had lost him, but instead of taking the next turn leading to our house, he asked me to turn the opposite way.

"Where are we going?"

"If it is Arno, there's only one place I know where he won't follow us."

I immediately caught his train of thought and took the next turn without any instruction. We ended up in a small neighborhood just south of downtown. After a few more turns, we pulled into the small driveway and parked next to an empty patrol car. Just as Marco met me by the driver's door, we saw a dark colored vehicle creeping along the adjacent street, before turning on its lights and speeding away.

Marie Baker opened the door with a pleasantly surprised expression. She let us in, quietly thanked us and then voiced her concerns about her fiancés behavior. "I can't get him to eat. He won't leave the basement. I've never seen him like this."

She led us down the stairs and into the furnished basement. The clapboard walls were decorated with police plaques and honorary awards. There were also framed pictures of previous officer classes, old family portraits and several newer photographs of him and Marie. She knocked on the opened door to a makeshift office where Reilly was seated with his back to us. He turned around and took off his reading glasses.

"What are you doing here?" he asked.

Marco answered, "We think someone's following us."

Reilly came out and slumped down in an old recliner. The basement furniture looked as though it had come straight out of the seventies. Marco and I sat on the rust-colored couch and Marie offered to make drinks at the small basement bar.

"Do you know who?" Reilly asked.

"We don't know for sure, but it looks like an unmarked police car," Marco said. "It could be a private investigator I know, or it could be Arno."

"I wouldn't be surprised," Reilly huffed. "Did he follow you here?"

"Almost," I answered. "but then he took off."

Reilly looked stumped. "Why would he be following you?"

"Because we have something he wants," I said and then looked at Marco. "He must have been waiting for Darlene to come home so he could ambush her, force his way inside and make her find those cameras."

Marie came back with several drinks and took a seat next to Reilly. They both listened intently as I continued. "We talked to Darlene Cutler and she told us that Dylan is being used as Arno's personal criminal informant. He's been harassed and physically abused by Arno in the past, so they set up cameras to catch him in the act. Dylan must have thought that something incriminating is on one of those files, and if Arno knows that we have the video evidence, he's going to want it back."

"How would he know?" Reilly asked.

"He overheard me talking to Dylan at the jail," I said. "I'm sure he knows."

"We can't let him get that evidence," Reilly insisted. "I can escort you to the station and hand it over to the captain."

I stopped him. "Sean, why would Arno spend all this energy trying to put an innocent boy behind bars? He has Luke in custody, and proof that he was lying about his alibi. Why go after Dylan?"

Reilly shook his head. "He obviously doesn't have enough evidence to convict Luke, because they released him this evening."

The information quickly absorbed and the weight of the situation began taking its toll on my neck. I rolled my shoulders and tried to relax as Reilly and Marco continued discussing the investigation. Even if the video evidence could prove Dylan was not the killer, we still had to somehow put Luke at the scene of the crime.

Marie and I chatted for a moment before Reilly asked about the mysterious bag of apples. The scene instantly flashed through my mind and a thought occurred to me.

"Dylan isn't completely innocent." I said, stopping the conversation dead in its tracks. "I think I know what happened."

The three of them listened as I began piecing the final clues together. "Dylan went across the street to the Rafferty's house and Paige gave him a bag of apples for his mom, but he didn't leave right away. Maybe he heard Luke knock on the back door, or they were interrupted, but Dylan stuck around to see what was happening. He could have been right on the opposite side of that fence watching through the window when I knocked and scared Luke away."

"Then Dylan would have had to sneak back into the house and steal her stuff before the cops showed up," Marco said, trying to find a weak spot in my theory, as good detectives always do.

"Yes," I agreed. "So let's say he dropped the bag of apples in the bushes, jumped the gate to the backyard and witnessed the entire thing. There was plenty of time, at least five minutes, for Dylan to get into the house and steal some of her valuables after I knocked. He could have taken off out the back door just like Luke did and doubled back to his mom's house. But there was one thing that Dylan couldn't have stolen."

"Her phone," Marco finished for me, "with a brand new crystal cell phone cover. Luke must have

133

dropped it in the street, causing some the crystals to fall off, before picking it up and peeling away."

"And that's when her phone was tracked to Miller's trucking firm," Reilly concluded.

"Exactly," I said. "It all makes sense."

"Then we need to get those video files over to the station and have the captain look at them," Reilly said. "We'll make sure that Dylan can give a statement without Arno around. With Dylan's testimony and those videos, we could have enough evidence to get Luke convicted and Detective Arno kicked off the force for good."

"That sounds like a plan to me," I said.

Reilly smiled. "Me too." His cell phone began to ring and he answered, making his way back into his office as we continued talking.

"We just better hope those files hold some incriminating evidence," Marco said.

"I think they do," I replied. "Why else would Dutch be following us?"

Marie interjected. "Do you think Sean will be reinstated if this is all true?"

Marco answered, "If we can prove it, yes."

"I can't even begin to thank you," she said. "You have no idea how much this job means to him."

"I think I have some idea," I said with a smile.

Reilly rushed back out of his office with his police jacket in hand, "That was the tech specialist. Guess whose phone just turned back on?"

"You're kidding," I spouted. "Where is it?"

Reilly slipped on his jacket. "Miller's trucking firm."

"Luke might be destroying the evidence," I said, standing up.

Marco joined us on our feet. "Looks like we have a killer to catch."

The old Reilly I knew instantly came back to life. He rummaged through a drawer inside his office and pulled out a pair of handcuffs and a small sidearm. Marie gave him a kiss on the cheek before the three of us headed upstairs. Sean stepped into a pair of work boots and swiped a set of keys from the kitchen table. "I'll drive."

CHAPTER FOURTEEN

We sped down the highway under the dome of
swirling red and blue lights. The siren blared before us,
leaving a trail of sidelined cars in our wake. The trucking
firm where Luke stashed Paige's cell phone was a good
fifteen minutes down the highway, just outside city limits,
but we were making much faster time.

"I only know of one main entrance to Miller's
trucking," Reilly said loudly, "On the south side, off the
highway. When we take the exit, I'll turn off the siren and
go dark. We need to get the jump on him."

"Shouldn't we contact your officers," I asked from
the backseat, practically shouting over the siren and the
roaring engine, "so we can surround the place in case he
makes a run for it?"

"Not yet," he answered. "Dispatch will have to inform the Chief and he'll send the police after *me*, not Luke. I can't take that chance."

After an exhilarating race down the highway, Reilly exited and flipped a switch on his dash to cut the siren and then another to shut off the lights. Marco was in the passenger seat and I was in the back, separated by a thick Plexiglass window opened in the center so I could hear what they were saying.

"What do you want us to do?" Marco asked as Reilly made the turn toward Miller's.

"I need you both to keep your eyes peeled," he answered, now virtually whispering as the sheriff's patrol car crept along the service road, shrouded in darkness. "The last thing we want is a pursuit, so once we find the entrance, Marco, I want you to close it up and lock us in. If Luke's still here, we don't want him fleeing."

The trucking firm was enclosed by a tall, reinforced metal fence which ran around the wide perimeter of the building surrounding the cement lot. The entrance was locked up tight. Marco double checked that the fence couldn't be opened manually and jogged back to Reilly's car. "I don't think he got in this way."

"We'll check around back," Reilly said.

Marco and I scanned the area through the fence, but we weren't able to see much. There were tall security lamps scattered evenly throughout the lot, but most of the light was obscured by the oversized trucks parked in even rows surrounding the main building.

"He could be anywhere," I said.

"Look there." Marco pointed toward an open gate on the opposite side of the lot.

We drove quietly through the gate. Marco quickly jumped out of the car and slid the metal security fence closed behind us, latching it so that it could only be opened by hand. We then proceeded down a long stretch of gravel. As we came closer to the main building, I started moving between each of the rear windows, my eyes intently focused, searching under the trucks for any signs of Luke, but he was nowhere to be found.

Reilly passed Miller's front entrance, which was lit up under the bright lights of the company's fluorescent sign, and parked around the corner, where his car could be better concealed. In the large lot around us were trucks of all shapes and sizes, most of them semis, with different types of trailers for hauling building materials, transporting cars and livestock, and heavy industrial equipment.

"Listen to me carefully," Reilly said. "I don't want either of you to leave this vehicle." He looked at me in the rearview mirror. "That goes double for you, got it?" He waited until I nodded, then looked at Marco. "If you see something, flip these two switches. The lights and siren should scare away any trouble and I'll come running."

"What happens if you need help?" Marco asked.

"Help will be on the way." Reilly reached for the patrol radio, but before he could, we heard a tapping on the driver's side window.

Out of the darkness, Detective Richard Arno's face appeared through the glass. "I shouldn't be surprised," he stated as Reilly rolled the window down. "But I'm glad you're here, Sergeant. I could use your assistance."

"Why are you here?" Reilly asked cautiously.

"Same as you," he answered quietly. "I've had a tail on Luke all night. He's in the maintenance shed around back. Come with me."

138

Arno backed up, expecting Reilly to open the door and follow him, but I interrupted. "Don't go, Sean. Call dispatch and let them know where we are. Wait for backup."

"What are you waiting for?" Arno hurried him along. "We don't have much time."

"Something doesn't feel right," Marco said. "I think you should listen to Abby."

Arno approached the car again and leaned closer to look at us. "You two stay here. Luke might be armed. Come on, Sarge."

I locked my eyes onto Reilly's through the mirror and shook my head. My inner antenna was buzzing so strongly my hands were shaking. Reilly inhaled a deep breath and reached for the radio.

"Fine," Arno snarled. "Stay here like the coward you are. I'll go around back and do your job. I was always better at it anyway." He stepped away into the darkness and disappeared around the corner.

I could tell Reilly was struggling to keep his composure, but before I could think of the words to keep him from leaving, we heard two gunshots in the distance behind the building. Reilly sprang into action. He readied his holster and flipped the switch on his radio, "Call dispatch and give them our location. Give the code eleven ninety-nine." He was out of the car and around the corner before I could even repeat the code.

Marco did as Reilly instructed. He also thought to flip the switch that turned on the flashing emergency lights, further beckoning the coming Calvary. Then he turned to face me in the backseat. "Why is Arno here?"

139

"I don't know, Marco, because If he was tailing Luke all night, then who was following us from Darlene's house?"

"We need to find out," Marco said as he swiped open his home screen and began scrolling through his contacts. "Here we go, Vincent Wong." He tapped his number and put the phone on speaker. Chills raced up my arms as we waited, listening for any sounds of activity in between rings. The air around us was still and the far away buzzing of electric security lamps was all I could hear.

"Don't worry," Vince answered immediately, "I won't even begin to try your last name. What can I do for you, Marco?"

"Were you following us from Darlene's house?" he asked.

"Was I *following* you? Oh, come on. I admire you and all, but –"

"Yes or no, Vince."

"Nope," he answered cheerfully. "Still here at the Rafferty house."

Marco turned to look at me in the backseat with Vince still on the line. "Arno was following us from Darlene's house. Now he's here waiting for us. Could that be a coincidence?"

Before Marco could hang up I had an idea. "Ask him for Paige's cell number."

After a few moments of hearing Vince fiddle with his phone, he finally read aloud the digits to Paige's cell, which I then dialed into mine. "Thanks, Vince," I said.

Marco ended the call abruptly and exited the car. He opened my door and offered his hand. "Come on. Reilly's in danger."

We hurried in Reilly's footsteps under the cover of the building's roof. The red and blue lights spun silently, coating the surrounding darkness in a blur of purple shadows. Marco peered quickly around the corner and gave me the signal to stay put. After several seconds, Marco's hand went back up, signaling for me to follow. Around the corner was much more of the same, large trucks loaded with heavy equipment, but – surprise – no maintenance shed. We continued along in partial concealment and then stopped by the building's back door only to find it locked.

"Where are they?" I asked quietly.

Marco looked around, then crouched low, whispering over his shoulder "Why did you ask for Paige's number?"

I lowered myself behind an empty canister by the back door. "To call her phone and locate Luke."

"What if Luke's not here?" he asked.

"Who else would have turned on her phone?"

"Think about it, Abby. Doesn't this feel like a trap? Arno was at Darlene's house waiting to get that video evidence, but we took it. He followed us to Reilly's and no more than fifteen minutes later the phone turned on. That's exactly how long it would have taken for him to drive here. He lured us here to get those files."

"Then he would have had Paige's phone the whole time," I realized.

Marco nodded. "He's been tracking our every move. Somehow he's wrapped up in this murder and we've been on his trail ever since day one. That's why he's been threatening us."

And just like that the real scene played perfectly in front of my eyes. "Dylan didn't witness Luke at Paige's house." Thinking back to the fear in Dylan's voice when I mentioned Arno, and the terror I saw in his eyes when he saw the detective standing behind me at the jail, it all started to become clear, except for one thing. "Why would Dutch murder Paige Rafferty?"

"It doesn't matter right now," Marco said. "What matters are those files. Whatever Dylan caught on camera could blow this whole case wide open. When he realizes that Reilly doesn't have the files, he's going to come searching for us."

"What are we going to do? We can't leave Reilly."

"Call Paige's cell."

"Now?"

"Yes," he said and signaled for me to get lower.

I crouched behind him and unlocked my phone, the bright screen lighting my face in the dark. I pressed send and we waited, listening quietly. After what felt likes hours, I began to speak but Marco held up his finger.

"Do you hear that?" he asked.

There was a sound coming from across the lot, but it wasn't a ringtone. It sounded like the two men were arguing, or fighting. Then we heard a gunshot. I almost stumbled backwards, but Marco lifted me to my feet and we headed toward the sound.

I followed closely behind Marco as he crept forward through the rows of empty trucks, using them as cover. I could hear the two men fighting clearly then, and their shouting echoed throughout the lot. As we drew nearer, Marco stopped behind one of the semi beds. It was a flatbed trailer loaded with massive railroad car axles. I could smell the rust and metal as Marco leaned around the truck and I heard him say something under his breath.

"What is it?" I whispered.

Marco held me back. "Don't look."

But by that time it was too late. I shot forward into the light and saw Reilly just twenty feet in front of me, sprawled out on his back, the glow of the security lamp acting as a spotlight on his lifeless body. I sank back behind the truck, my knees caving, but as I did I heard the scraping of metal against metal and glanced around just as the trailer in front of us released its payload, the heavy, rusted objects rolling rapidly toward us.

I felt Marco's strong grip on my biceps as he desperately tried to pull me out of the way. But as he did, one of the railroad car axles toppled onto the ground next to me, colliding with another, flipping it end over end, and landed right on Marco's back. Before I could act, several more axles crashed onto the ground between us, one tearing into my arm as another crippled my leg, forcing me to the ground.

I looked behind me to see Marco face down, the weight of the axles crushing his back. He was struggling to breathe. I didn't have much time. I pulled my body forward, trying not to look at the gash on my arm, my palms shredding on the cold cement. The axle that held me down was resting on another, leaving a slight gap to pull my leg through. But as I did I could feel the skin on my leg peeling back, and a warm sensation running down my calf.

But the sensations at that point were nothing more than that because all I could hear was my pounding heartbeat and feel the blood pulsing through my veins as I tried desperately to help my husband.

I finally managed to free my leg and hobble next to Marco. He was conscious but gasping desperately for air. There were two axles on his back, one on top of the other. I gathered all my strength and rolled the first axle away. It

143

slammed to the ground next to us and I heard him inhale painfully.

"I'm here, Marco." I said, breathing hard. "Can you move at all?"

He pulled his arms underneath him as far as he could, almost completing a push-up position, but couldn't get them far enough under his body. "You have to help me," he said between gasping breaths. Marco pushed with what little strength remained, and I pulled, then feeling a searing pain rip through my arm.

"It's too heavy," I cried, my voice cracking from the strain. "I can't lift it."

"Remember," he said. His words were coming in quick short bursts. "Work through the pain."

I could tell he was losing his strength quickly and his breathing was slowing down. I closed my eyes, gritted my teeth, and bore down, gripping my hands so tightly around the axle that I lost feeling in them. The whole time Marco's words repeated inside my head. *Pain is all in the mind. Feel the burn.*

"You can do this, Abby," he said finally.

I felt the burn through my shoulders as I pulled. I felt every muscle fiber in my legs tighten as I pushed. The axle moved slightly, and Marco lifted his chin and drew in one large breath. I shifted my feet, inching the axle away from his shoulder blades, allowing him to pull his hands beneath his body and push. Together we lifted the axle enough for Marco to scoot forward, allowing the color to return to his cheeks.

I fell backward onto the pavement, my body as loose as a ragdoll's, but I didn't care. I could hear Marco breathing and coughing. He was alive.

144

I heard the crunching of gravel near my face and opened my eyes to see Richard Arno staring down at me. His face was contorted into a crooked smile. "You're a real hero, Abby Knight Salvare."

CHAPTER FIFTEEN

Arno put his hands on his hips, gazing down at me with his ugly smile. "I had so many people to hang this murder on, but I never expected it would be you." He snickered. "I guess you were right after all. I did railroad the first person I set my sights on."

"*You* killed Paige Rafferty," I said, pulling myself up. I stayed seated so I could see Marco, but Arno stepped in between us, blocking my view.

"Where are the files, Abby?"

"And you killed Reilly."

Arno looked over at Reilly who was still motionless on the ground. "He's not dead. He tried to shoot me and I clocked him one. Knocked him out cold. Weak chin I guess."

"How do you think this is going to end, Dutch?"

"Not well," he said. "Not well at all."

"How do you expect to get away with this? Are you going to frame all three of us?"

"It's not going to be easy, but I've had a lot of practice." He pulled his jacket back, once again revealing his service revolver holstered under his arm. "Let's see, disgraced ex-cop gone rogue. Two private investigators with nothing to lose. I can make it work."

Marco tried to speak. He was still partially pinned under the railroad axle. His face was scratched badly, but he was breathing steadily. He could hardly move to look up at Arno, but he tried.

"You stay put, hotshot," Arno said. "There's nothing left to do but hand over the files. Tell me where they are and maybe I'll let you live."

Marco's eyes fluttered closed again and his head dropped to one side.

Out of the corner of my eye I noticed Reilly's hand begin to move. I knew there was no way Arno could allow us to live. The only way out at that point was to stall him until the police showed up, or Reilly came to. I tried to shift Arno's focus solely onto me.

I turned to my husband and inched toward him, making a point to show how weak I was. Once Arno was facing away from Reilly, I continued. "You can't let us live, Dutch. I know that, but the least you can do is tell me why. Why did you murder Paige Rafferty?"

"Believe it or not, I don't want to kill you. You do good work. We're one in the same, you and me."

I accidentally laughed out loud. I couldn't help myself. "What makes you think we're the same?"

"I've been watching you for years," he said. "You don't give up." Arno bent down slightly and looked over my wounds, now bleeding profusely. "Look at you, still going. You're about to bleed to death and the only thing you want is to know the truth. Good for you, kid."

"I know you killed her, Dutch."

"You call me Dutch one more time and I *will* put a bullet in you," he said between gritted teeth. He stood up looked back at Reilly, who was still lying face up on the pavement. "Tell me, how do you know that I was the one who killed her?" he asked. "What proof do you have?"

I knew what he was getting at. He wanted me to confess that I had the video files, but I wouldn't give it up. I put my hand on Marco's face, then pulled my purse from around my body, the video files still secured in the outside pocket, and used it to cushion Marco's head from the ground. "I don't have any proof, but the evidence all points to you."

He gave me a mocking laugh. "Evidence and proof are two very different things. I learned that the hard way, but like I said, I never make the same mistake twice. I leave nothing to chance, and once you're out of the way, there's only one person responsible for closing this case. Me." He reached his hand for his gun in an attempt to threaten me once again. "Tell me where they are."

"Tell me why you murdered Paige."

"You don't hold the cards here," he shouted. "Where are the files?"

"Did you even have a plan?" I asked. "Because it seems like you didn't have one at all. You stumbled from one suspect to another. You planted evidence and threatened people to confess. What kind of plan is that? You're supposed to be the best detective in town."

"The only kink in my plan," he said as he drew his weapon. "Was you."

"You are the worst detective," I continued. "You're not even good at planting evidence, let alone finding it. How many people did you have to frame, three? And you still couldn't get it right."

"How could I when you show up at my heels every step of the way?" His words came out in flames as he directed his anger at me. "This plan was airtight. Slade Rafferty murders his wife, stages the robbery, done. Guilty. But then here comes Abby Knight, the florist, knocking on that door as I'm staging the damn house. There goes the husband theory, so then I turn to Luke, hiding his phone in this dump, all ready to take the fall, until I see you two nosing around at the bar. There goes that plan. Then you show up looking for Dylan and what do you know, the snitch is about to snitch on me." He put his hands on his hips and laughed. "You just can't trust anybody these days."

"How could you do this? You are supposed to be protecting people."

His indignant smile dropped sharply as Arno turned toward his old friend and partner. "Ask your Sergeant," he finally answered. "He knows how the system works. He let a guilty man walk free because of a technicality. How is that protecting people?"

I saw Reilly slowly sit up and hold his head, but didn't focus my attention for very long as Arno continued.

"While I informed the parents that the man who murdered their daughter was going to live out the rest of his life as a free man, Sean Reilly was receiving a commendation and a promotion. All I had to do was plant that school book and Barnes would be rotting in jail right now."

"Is that your justification for breaking the law? You get more convictions than anyone, but how much of it is actually the truth?"

"The system doesn't always work. That's the truth. But I go to work every damn day. I see criminals get away on technicalities all the time. How is that right? Justice shouldn't have technicalities. I simply swing the balance back onto our side. Do you have any idea how many people would have gotten away with their crimes if I hadn't been there to nudge the truth every once in a while? The truth isn't always black or white, Ms. Detective. True justice is dirty. I live in between the lines. I get results."

"You ruin people's lives."

He laughed. "Are you talking about Luke, the abusive drunk, or Dylan, the thieving drug addict? How long before one of them ruins someone else's life? What's so bad about getting these people off the streets for good?"

"Yes," I answered. "I'm talking about Luke and Dylan, but also Slade and Paige Rafferty. You took her life and ruined his. And what about Sergeant Reilly? He was your best friend. He's a better cop than you'll ever be, Dutch. You hurt innocent people."

"You're right," he said as he pointed the barrel at my chest. "Paige Rafferty didn't deserve to die, and Sean Reilly was my best friend, but here's another piece of truth." He pulled back the hammer on his revolver. "No one is truly innocent in this world."

I closed my eyes just before the shot rang out and the percussion blasted by my ear. The explosion echoed throughout the empty lot and for the next few seconds all

I could hear was the high-pitched tone that seemed to pierce my skull.

I opened my eyes to see Arno clutch his right shoulder, then heard another loud pop as he fell to his knees, the revolver hanging upside down on his trigger finger. He looked at me, his face turning white as I watched the blood soak through the shoulder of his dark brown trench coat. Arno fell to the ground in front of me, and under the lamp light I saw Sergeant Sean Reilly, still standing firm in his firing position, smoke rising from the barrel of his pistol.

Reilly came up from behind and secured the gun, lowered Arno onto his stomach and began cuffing him. "Save your speech for the jury, Detective."

As Arno desperately submitted under Reilly, I turned to my husband. I was beginning to feel lightheaded, the adrenaline wearing off and the bleeding from my arm and leg starting to take effect. Reilly joined me and together we lifted the heavy axle from Marco's back. Sean then produced a white handkerchief from his back pocket and tightened it around my leg.

We moved Marco onto his back and he came to, his eyelids slowly opening as we heard the distant sounds of sirens. Arno was still flailing and cursing at us, but it was just noise at that point. I sat down next to Marco and caressed his face.

Still handsome, even with the tousled hair, scratched face and bruised eye, my husband looked up at me and smiled. "Nice form, Sunshine" he said and tried to laugh. "You saved me."

"I had to," I replied, then leaned down to give him a kiss. "I'm not spending an entire week alone on that cruise with my family."

As Reilly pulled Arno to his knees we heard a small cracking sound on the ground behind us. I limped closer and noticed Paige's cell phone had fallen from Detective Arno's coat pocket. On the ground next to the pink case were a few scattered crystals.

"I would say that's a very convincing piece of evidence," I said.

Arno didn't say a word. He just curled his upper lip and glared at me with disgust.

Several police cars and two ambulances arrived on the scene. As Reilly and I were given initial assessments, Marco was put onto a stretcher. The medical techs were ready to wrap me in some heavy duty bandages, but I asked to sit with Marco first.

As the EMTs helped me over to the stretcher, I saw Captain Fontaine speaking with Reilly, so I said to Marco, "I'll be right back." Marco lifted his head, his neck secured with a stiff brace, and managed a wink. I blew him a kiss and met up with Reilly and Fontaine, gathered around Arno's stretcher, which was still resting on the ground near the second ambulance as the medical techs wrapped his wounds. From my purse, I pulled the video files and Arno scoffed, still clinging to his innocence.

"That proves nothing," Arno said. "This town will fall to pieces without me. I've solved twenty murder cases in that past five years. No one pulls those kinds of numbers."

"This town will be just fine without you," I said. The stretcher lifted off the ground and Detective Richard Arno kept his eyes locked onto mine as they raised to meet me. "Because as of right now, Dutch, we just solved twenty-one."

"You and me, kid. Were the same. How long until you need justice so bad that you blur the lines just enough to cross them? "

"Justice shouldn't have technicalities," I admitted. "You're right about that, but there is a line I will never cross."

"I thought the same thing once." Arno laughed and coughed, his chest restrained by the straps. "But you will cross that line one day. And I won't blame you when you do."

I patted the stretcher with a smile. "Take him away boys."

Reilly stood proudly next to me and we watched Dutch squirm in place and swear as he was loaded into the ambulance. "Take him away, boys?" Sean asked. "Was that really necessary?"

"No, but it sounded cool. Didn't it?"

He folded his arms and gave me a look, but before he could answer I said, "Come on, Sarge. Let me have this one. I'm feeling pretty good right now."

"You got it, Detective."

. . .

My staff from Bloomers made sure our hospital rooms were fully decorated with the most beautiful bouquets the shop had to offer. After several days laid up the hospital, and numerous visits from staff, family, and police, Marco and I were released to finish our recovery at home. My muscles still ached, and the sutures under my

153

bandages throbbed, but it was a good feeling, a reminder of my accomplishments. Had it not been for the last two weeks of painfully intensive workout sessions, who knows if I would have the strength to save Marco, mentally or physically.

We were both relaxing in the living room when the doorbell rang. I looked at my husband, reclining on the sofa, petting our giant Russian Blue nestled on his lap while also stroking our little mutt, Seedy, stretched out on the sofa next to him. "I guess I'll get it." I stood and groaned in agony, slowly making my way to the front door.

I opened it to see Reilly and his fiancé standing there.

"You look about how I feel," Reilly said, as I let them both in. His cheek was black and blue and his eye was dark and puffy.

I offered to get drinks, but Marie insisted that she make them for us, assuring me she knew her way around a kitchen. Reilly let out a sigh as he settled down next to Seedy on the couch. Marco gave him a nod then winced at the movement but I was all smiles, even with nearly half my body wrapped in bandages. I sat down on the chair across from Sean and Marco, the three of us making quite a frightening sight. We sat in silence for a few moments, finally rejoined after our harrowing night at the truck yard.

I leaned in across from Sean and Marco. "Well, Sarge, fill us in."

"It's not Sarge yet," he corrected. "There's a long review process before I'm allowed back to work."

"He's in no hurry," Marie called from the kitchen. "He deserves a little time to heal."

"That reminds me," I said. "What happened after you left the car with Arno?"

"I followed him out into the parking lot, but I was careful. I had my gun drawn, and stayed behind him. That's when I heard Paige's phone ring."

"How did you know it was her phone?" I asked.

Sean thought for a moment before answering. "I had an idea what he was up to, but I guess being friends with him all those years, when that phone rang I knew what he had done. I told him to put his hands up, but he came at me, violently."

"Has he confessed yet?" Marco asked.

"No," Reilly answered. "And I doubt he ever will. He knows how it works. He's going to deny it until the day he dies, no matter what kind of proof we have."

"What about the files?" I asked. "Did Dylan catch anything incriminating on those cameras?"

"He sure did."

Marie came into the room with our drinks. She handed them out as Reilly thanked her and continued, "Turns out Dylan didn't steal Paige's laptop or wedding ring. The camera in Dylan's bedroom showed Detective Arno planting those items under his bed, and then showed the same scene several hours later when he came back with two officers, who found the evidence and arrested Dylan."

"I'm assuming Dylan's been released," I said.

"Eventually he was, but not before we got the full story out of him. It doesn't matter now if Arno ever confesses because Dylan witnessed the whole thing."

Marie sat down in the chair next to me and we listened as Reilly told us the full story.

"Dylan was at the Rafferty's house and the scene played out just as you had imagined, Abby, but when he saw Arno at the back door he knew something was wrong. It turns out that Arno had been visiting Dylan way more often than he needed, because he had his eye on Paige Rafferty.

"According to Dylan, she spent a lot of time outside tending to the yard and garden after marrying Slade, according to witnesses. Arno was at the Cutler's house for information about the neighborhood robberies when he first saw Paige across the street. We think that he used the robberies as an excuse to get near her. After that, Arno would visit Dylan daily, leaving his car parked in front of the Cutler's house while slipping across the street to see her."

"Was there something going on between them?" I asked.

"We don't know for sure," Reilly answered. "But we do know that there were no signs of sexual assault before the murder."

"Everyone we talked to said Paige couldn't say no to anyone," I said.

"A slick talking, persuasive detective would be a very hard man to turn away," Marco added.

"We found phone records between Arno and Paige," Reilly said, "but they were one way. He called her, but she had never once called him. We also know that Arno called Slade Rafferty the morning of the murder and set up a phony appointment under the guise of being a prospective home buyer, making sure he was away when Arno visited Paige.

"My theory is that she finally turned down Arno's advances," Reilly continued. "She may have threatened to call her husband or the police when he wouldn't leave and that must have set him off. We're guessing he choked her before she could make the call then pocketed her phone. If

156

you hadn't been there to stop him staging the crime scene, Abby, he might have gotten away with it, too."

"So Dylan was just an innocent bystander," I said. "He was caught in the middle."

"Right," Sean agreed. "He was afraid if he didn't confess to the murder, Arno would send him back to prison and let everyone know he was working as an informant. That was enough of a threat to keep Dylan quiet. And the kid admitted he was very close to accepting the blame, as well. That's how scared he was. He said Arno made it very clear what happens to snitches in prison."

"What about Luke?" Marco asked. "How was he involved?"

Reilly took a long sip of his drink and answered, "Arno knew about him as well. He's a good detective, I'll admit that. He dug into Paige's past and found every person he could frame for this crime. Luckily, we didn't give him enough time to do it properly. You two really saved the day."

"We can't thank you enough," Marie said. "In fact, we want to do something special in return." She glanced at her fiancé, who was beginning to blush. "Do you want to ask them?"

Reilly shook his head, a secretive smile on his face. "You do it."

Marie turned to us with a smile as she smoothed the fabric around her belly, revealing a tiny baby bump. "We'd like you to be the godparents of our firstborn. We can't think of anyone more worthy."

A wide smile spread across my face as I looked at Marco, whose face was too bruised to show much emotion. "Of course we will," I said. "It would be our honor."

Marie and I stood and I gave her a long hug.

From over her shoulder I watched as Sargent Sean Reilly extended his hand to my husband. Marco proudly stiffened his jaw and reached his hand over, clasping together in a strong shake. "Congrats, Sarge," Marco said.

Just then the doorbell rang. "You two need to stick around for a while," I said eagerly. "My mom and dad are bringing over lots of food, and Marco's family is coming over as well. We'll have a get-well party."

Sean and Marco both had looks of exasperation on their faces, but Marie was all smiles. "That sounds lovely."

I hobbled into the hallway, more out of habit than necessity. I was healing quickly, but I wasn't prepared for who I saw when I opened the door.

Jillian stood before me in full workout attire, a yoga mat under one arm and a large rubber ball under the other. She stared me straight in the eyes and said, without hesitation, "You, me, Pilates…now."

THE END

DEDICATION

I would like to thank my daughter, Julia, for her dedication to family. I know in my heart that, no matter what, she will always be at my side. I was a teacher before having children, but after having her, I became the student. Thank you, sweetheart.

I would also like to thank my son, Jason, my hard-working, creative assistant and personal publicist, for his dedication and crusade to keep the flower shop mysteries alive and thriving. Thank you, Jason.

Other Flower Shop Mysteries

MUM'S THE WORD
SLAY IT WITH FLOWERS
DEARLY DEPOTTED
SNIPPED IN THE BUD
ACTS OF VIOLETS
A ROSE FROM THE DEAD
SHOOTS TO KILL
EVIL IN CARNATIONS
SLEEPING WITH ANEMONE
DIRTY ROTTEN TENDRILS
NIGHT OF THE LIVING DANDELION
TO CATCH A LEAF
NIGHTSHADE ON ELM STREET
SEED NO EVIL
THROW IN THE TROWEL
A ROOT AWAKENING
FLORIST GRUMP
MOSS HYSTERIA
YEWS WITH CAUTION
MISSING UNDER THE MISTLETOE - NOVELLA

Continue reading for a special *first look* at
The Goddess of Greene Mysteries

STATUE OF LIMITATIONS

GODDESS OF GREENE MYSTERIES

BY KATE COLLINS

Preface

IT'S ALL GREEK TO ME
Blog by Goddess Anon
Chaos Reigns

Talk about chaos. First of all, I come from a big, noisy- and nosy- Greek family consisting of several annoying siblings, a meddling mother firmly committed to the idea that I should marry a nice Greek boy, a father who, although not fully Greek, has totally embraced the culture, and my grandparents Pappoús *(or Pappou, as we say, and* Yaya *(actually it's spelled Oiaoiá, but you'd have a hard time pronouncing that.).*

Secondly, when I was young I prayed for a handsome white knight to come along to rescue me, and guess what? Nothing. Ever. Happened. I finally figured out I'd have to do it myself. So, at the ripe old age of twenty-four, I packed a suitcase, moved to the closest big city, got a studio apartment, a low-paying job at a big corporation and worked my way up until I reached a level of success that made me happier than I'd ever dreamed possible.

I also married a very successful, non-Greek businessman, which caused all kinds of uproar back home. So along with a wedding gift, my mother gave me three pieces of advice: the man you're marrying will break your heart; you'll never be able to support yourself alone in the city; and then you'll come back home where you belong.

Oh, how I prayed that she would be wrong but, once again, my prayers went unanswered, because, much to my consternation, it turned out that she was right.

Ten years later, after unchaining myself from a bitter marriage from a husband who left me in debt up to my ears, with my corporate job eliminated and a young child to support, I had to pack up our belongings, along with my pride, and return back home into the welcoming arms of my family.

Now my child and I not only live in the big family house, but I also work for the family business, which at least enables me to earn my own money, so I can move into my own place one day. In the meantime, my child, who'd been so distraught by the divorce, does seem to be blossoming here in the midst of our eccentric but strong fam—

CHAPTER ONE

Monday 8:10 p.m.

My computer monitor flickered briefly, and the screen went black. The lights in the ceiling high above my desk made a buzzing sound and then they, too, went dark. The window beside my desk offered little help. The bright May sun had set fifteen minutes ago.

Muttering under my breath, I reached for my cell phone only to remember that I'd set it on the dark wood console table on the opposite side of my office. A bolt of lightning momentarily illuminated the room, enabling me to make my way around the old oak desk and across the wood floor to the table. At a sudden heavy Pappoús' thud from somewhere outside my office, I paused. Standing in the dark at the foot of the table, I waited, listening.

Hearing nothing more, I did a quick mental inventory. My mother and father, who owned *Spencer's Garden Center*, and my youngest sister Delphi, had left when the shop closed at eight. I'd flipped over the CLOSED

166

sign and locked the door myself. I had made sure that there was no one around so I could release some pent-up frustrations through my blog. So what had caused the noise?

I located my phone, switched on the flashlight, and shined it at the open doorway. Thunder rumbled in the distance as I quietly made my way out of the office at the front of the shop next to the L-shaped checkout counter. Over a century ago the garden center had been a barn, but a brand new arched roof, high-beamed ceiling, cream-colored shiplap walls, and a shiny oak floor had turned it into one of the most attractive shops on Greene Street.

Fortunately, nothing seemed out of place – the cash register hadn't been touched, the bolt on the red barn entrance doors was still thrown, nothing on any of the shelves had been disturbed, none of the garden decor on the walls was askew, and no windows had been broken.

Another thud turned me in the direction of the outdoor garden area, located on a half-acre lot behind the barn, and then I had my answer. It was undoubtedly Oscar, our friendly neighborhood raccoon, who liked to steal shiny objects at night. He'd ruined any number of items in the back area where we kept garden decor, and I wasn't about to let him ruin another one.

Using the cellphone's flashlight as my guide, I headed toward the rear exit. Circling the patio table section, I pushed the glass door open and stepped outside just as the electricity came back on. Hanging lanterns around the perimeter illuminated the entire area, one side filled with rows of flowering plants, a fruits and vegetable section and the other with stone, clay, glass and cement sculptures, water fountains, decorative planters, wrought iron benches and outdoor wall decor.

I caught movement from the corner of my eye and backed against the door with a sharp gasp.

A man was crouched at the base of a life-sized marble statue of the Goddess Athena, now lying on her back in the grass. He had an open pocketknife in his hand and his cell phone was propped nearby, its flashlight aimed at the statue's base. He jumped to his feet, obviously as shocked to see me as I was to see him.

"Drop that knife and don't move a muscle." I thrust my phone forward, the beam pointed at his face and my trembling finger on the home button. "I've got the police on the line."

If only that were true.

The lights flickered, threatening to go out again.

"Okay," he said in a calm voice. "No problem." Moving slowly, he placed the knife on the ground and raised his hands above his head. "I'm sorry. I didn't mean to alarm you."

"You broke into our shop. What did you *think* that would do to me?"

"Hold on a minute," he said in a voice rising in panic. "I did *not* break into the shop. I was *told* to stay here until someone could help me, and that was" –he tipped his wrist to see his watch- "over twenty minutes ago."

I gave him a skeptical glance. "You've been out here for twenty minutes?"

"*Over* twenty minutes. Again, I'm sorry for alarming you, but I was just doing what I was told."

Undeniably good looking, the man had wavy dark hair that brushed the tops of his ears and down around the collar of his tan suede bomber jacket. He had big golden-brown eyes, a firm mouth, and a strong jawline that drew my gaze in and down to his muscular shoulders and athletic build. He was wearing dark blue jeans with the jacket, noticeably expensive navy leather loafers, and an expression that seemed to say he was sincere.

But I was alone with a stranger in the back of an empty shop on Greene Street, the main thoroughfare of our small coastal town, with only my phone and my wits to protect me. The other shops had closed and any tourists who'd stuck around would no doubt be comfortably seated inside a restaurant or one of the local sports bars. With the storm quickly approaching, who would hear me cry for help?

I jumped at a sudden clap of thunder. With all the bravery I could muster, still holding my phone, I pointed toward the small lane that ran behind our property. "You need to leave right now."

"Will you at least give me a chance to prove I'm telling the truth? If you don't believe me, I'll go."

A strong eastern wind blew through the garden area, shifting the hanging lanterns, and causing my long, blue sweater to billow out around my white pants. I could smell the rain coming.

Brushing long strands of light brown hair away from my face, I said, "Make it fast."

"The young woman who waited on me -- I didn't get her name -- is probably in her late twenties, with lots of black hair, very curly, tied back with some kind of fuzzy purple thing. She had on a purple sweater, jeans, and bright green flip-flops. flats. She was shorter than you but had more. . ." He gave me a sweeping glance, his eyes moving from my fair, straight hair all the way down to my white flats. He saw the narrowing of my gaze, and finished with, "color in her cheeks."

169

That wasn't what he'd meant to say and we both knew it. He had just described Delphi, my airhead of a sister who, like my other two sisters Maia and Selene, had the curvaceous bodies and olive complexions of my Greek-American mother, Hera Karras Spencer. I, on the other hand, was the only one who had inherited the paler, slender form and straight brown hair of Alexander Spencer, my half-Greek half-English father.

It was quite likely that Delphi had gotten busy with something else and had forgotten to tell me about the stranger. Her absentmindedness was common enough to convince me the man could be telling the truth, but still, what did he intend to do with that knife?

I gestured toward the statue. "What were you doing?"

"Can I put my hands down? My arms are tired."

I gave him a curt nod.

"Thank you. I'm Case Donnelly by the way."

As he walked closer, holding out his hand to shake mine, I realized I was still clutching my cell phone.

"You might want to put that away." His mouth quirked as though trying to hide a grin. "I'm guessing the police hung up a long time ago or they'd have been here by now."

I stood my ground, my gaze locked with his.

"And your flashlight app is on, by the way."

He wasn't missing a trick. Feeling an embarrassing blush creep up my face, I turned off the app, slid the phone in my back pocket, and took his hand. "Athena Spencer," I said in a crisp, business-like voice. I'd gone back to my maiden name when the divorce became final.

"Athena." He looked impressed. "Like your *Treasure of Athena*."

170

That he knew the statue's name surprised me since it wasn't written on any tag.

"It's a pleasure to meet you, Athena. Are you the owner here?"

His charming smile and warm, firm grip left me a little breathless. I dropped his hand and stepped back, feeling awkward and at the same time angry with him for causing it. "I'm the business manager. My parents own the garden center. Now would you answer my question, please?"

"I'd be glad to." He gestured toward the overturned figure. "I was trying to find out if the statue is authentic."

"She's authentic."

"Do you have the legal paperwork to prove it?"

Feeling my temper on the rise I said, "Yes. It's called a sales receipt."

"And does it say on this sales receipt that the statue is by the Greek sculptor Antonius?"

I paused to think. Had I seen the name Antonius anywhere on the information I'd filed away? Who was Antonius anyway?

As though reading my thoughts Case said, "Antonius is a Roman artist from the early twelfth century who became famous posthumously for his sculptures of Greek gods and goddesses."

I lifted my chin. "As a matter of fact, I do know that." *Not.* "And anyway, it doesn't matter. The statue isn't for sale."

"That's okay. I wasn't interested in buying it. But just out of curiosity, may I see the receipt?"

His impertinence irritated me. "No, you may not. It's late, I'm hungry, and I was supposed to meet someone for dinner ten minutes ago."

Case studied me with a shrewdness that made me uneasy. "It's just after eight o'clock. Why isn't the garden center open?"

"All of the shops close at eight. You're not from around here, are you?"

Completely ignoring my question, he glanced back at the statue. "I'm betting you paid a lot of money for her."

His sudden switch of topics threw me off guard. Plus, I was growing hungrier – and angrier – by the second. I hadn't wanted to eat dinner this late, but of course, when did my wishes count?

"First of all, I didn't buy the statue. My grandfather did. Secondly, how much he paid isn't your concern. Now would you please keep your promise and leave?"

"I'll take that as a yes, she did cost a lot of money. I hope your grandfather at least bought her from a reputable art dealer."

"Not that it's any of your business, but he bought her at an estate sale." Why had I told him that?

My stomach rumbled, reminding me why.

"So an auctioneer sold it to him, did he? Is the auction house reliable?"

I balled my hands into fists, not about to admit that neither the auctioneer nor the auction house was one I knew anything about.

"Okay," he said, "I'll mark that down as a *you don't know*. Whose estate was up for auction?"

I pulled my cell phone out of my pocket. "Get out now or I really will call the police."

"One more question. Did the auctioneer inform your grandfather that someone had applied a thin layer of cement over the bottom of the statue where the sculptor's name should be?"

I glanced in surprise at the sandal-clad feet of the marble Athena and saw that Case had indeed scraped off a bit of what appeared to be a cement coating.

"I'll take that as no," he said. "Therefore, my question for you is, why would someone put cement over the sculptor's name unless it wasn't a genuine Antonius?"

I absorbed the information with a sinking feeling in the pit of my stomach. Had my pappoús been ripped off?

Case straightened his jacket cuffs, clearly satisfied that he'd made his point.

And indeed, he had. With one eye on the black clouds overhead I asked, "How long will it take you to find out if she's authentic?"

"Five minutes, and I won't even charge you for my services."

I stared at him in surprise.

Case smiled, revealing a charming dimple in his cheek. "I'm joking."

His teasing helped break the tension between us, and I couldn't help but smile back. I glanced at my watch. "All right, Case Donnelly, you've got five minutes."

As he crouched down to work, my nerves kicked in. What if this outrageously expensive piece of art was a fake, not even worth the price it had cost to move it from the Talbot's estate to our diner? I felt sick to my stomach thinking about it.

When I'd learned that my grandfather had planned to purchase the statue at an estate auction, I'd protested mightily that it was too big for the average customer's garden and too far out of their budget anyway.

But as usual my voice went unheard. The family had gathered behind my stubborn Pappoús because he was the head of the family and his decisions were final, regardless of what the *business manager* had to say.

It wasn't until the family had to come up with the money to buy it that Pappoús had realized he'd gotten us in over our heads. But by then it was too late. Now we were stuck with it until we could convince Pappoús we needed to sell it.

As Case worked, I had to admit that the *Treasure of Athena* was beautiful. I hadn't seen such exquisite detail in a marble sculpture since I'd toured museums with my family in Greece years ago.

Standing at over six-feet tall, the statue Athena wore a traditional flowing toga, gathered over one shoulder with a clasp so that the material draped down over her small, firm breasts. Another layer of material swirled down from her waist to the sandals on her feet. Her hair was swept up beneath a helmet that covered the top of her head. Her arms were bare and slender, but her strength was evident. One hand rested on her right hip, the other hand was outstretched in greeting.

Case blew away the dust he'd scraped off, uncovering a small brass plate attached to the bottom of one of Athena's soles. I knelt down for a closer look as he wiped off the brass with his palm. "There's your marking."

I squinted at the etching but couldn't make sense of it. "Is that in Greek?"

"You don't read Greek?"

"I skipped Greek school. Does that mean the statue's an authentic Antonius?"

"She's authentic, all right, and worth a small fortune."

As he hoisted the sculpture back to its standing position, I stared at it in awe, my heart racing as the words *small fortune* echoed in my head. We owned an authentic Greek Antonius? Surely Pappoús wouldn't mind selling now. And just think what they could do with that money to spruce up the interior of their outdated diner.

Case held out a hand to help me up. "There's one more thing you should know about her, Athena."

"And that is?"

He brushed dirt off the statue's exquisite marble face. "She's mine."

ABOUT THE AUTHOR

Kate Collins is the author of the best-selling Flower Shop Mystery series. Her books have made the New York Times Bestseller list, the Barnes & Noble mass market mystery best-sellers' lists, the Independent Booksellers' best-seller's lists, as well as booksellers' lists in the U.K. and Australia. The first three books in the FSM series are now available on audiobook. Kate's new series, GODDESS OF GREENE MYSTERIES, will be available in 2019.

In January of 2016, Hallmark Movies & Mysteries channel aired the first Flower Shop Mystery series movie, MUM'S THE WORD, followed by SLAY IT WITH FLOWERS and DEARLY DEPOTTED. The movies star Brooke Shields, Brennan Elliott, Beau Bridges and Kate Drummond.

Kate started her career writing children's stories for magazines and eventually published historical romantic suspense novels under the pen name Linda Eberhardt and Linda O'brien. Seven romance novels later, she switched to her true love, mysteries.

Made in the USA
San Bernardino, CA
03 August 2018